The Darkness Within

Against the Darkness 3

H. L. Wegley

Suspense

Publisher's Note: This is a work of fiction set in a real location. Any reference to historical figures, places, or events, whether fictional or actual, is a fictional representation. Names, characters, and incidents are the product of the author's imagination or are used fictitiously, and any resemblance to actual persons, living or dead, or events is entirely coincidental.

Cover Font: Jason Walcott
http://www.onlinewebfonts.com

ISBN-13: 978-1-7344890-9-5
ISBN-10: 1-7344890-9-X

Also available in ebook publication

Dedication

Darkness is assaulting America in many forms and is now bringing persecution to those who stand against the darkness. This book is dedicated to those pastors and other church leaders in their congregations who stand strong and shine the light of truth into ***the darkness within***. As the cost of following Jesus grows, we need men and women willing to stand shoulder-to-shoulder with our brothers and sisters to encourage them, provide for their needs, protect them, pray for righteousness, liberty, and justice to prevail in our nation, and to vote accordingly. May God bless you as you do these things.

Acknowledgments

Thanks to my wife, Babe, for making *The Darkness Within* a better story by listening to me read her the novel to catch plot holes and any logical errors.

Thanks to the doctors, journalists, and watchdog organizations who risked their careers to expose *The Darkness Within* the healthcare system and industry in the United States. It is these folks who made this story possible.

And, of course, I thank my Heavenly Father for leaving me enough words and wits to finish another novel.

Contents

"The case against science is straightforward: much of the scientific literature, perhaps half, may simply be untrue. Afflicted by studies with small sample sizes, tiny effects, invalid exploratory analyses, and flagrant conflicts of interest, together with an obsession for pursuing fashionable trends of dubious importance, ***science has taken a turn towards darkness****."*

Richard Horton, Editor-in-Chief, The Lancet

For we do not wrestle against flesh and blood, but against principalities, against powers, ***against the rulers of the darkness of this age****, against spiritual hosts of wickedness in the heavenly places.*

Ephesians 6:12 (NKJV)

Chapter 1

May 31st, 8:00 a.m. MDT, Meiling and Ryan's apartment in Dr. Pierce's lab compound near Superior, Colorado

The international battle against the Marburg Pandemic had held its own for the past six weeks using Dr. Meiling Chen-Adams's therapeutics as the primary defense weapons. Though Meiling and Ryan had not forgotten this deadly evil propagated by the Chinese Communist Party (CCP), they had agreed to turn their attention to the darkness within the United States government and the healthcare industry. This darkness had become the biggest threat to the light of freedom in America.

The Department of Health and Human Services (DHHS) and the large pharmaceutical companies, often assisted by the U.S. Department of Justice, had harassed and hindered Meiling as she sought to manage President Warrington's Marburg response. But the time had come to expose the evil, power- and money-mongers who had proven willing to watch people die if it gave them opportunities to gain power and profit.

President Warrington had warned Meiling that the government healthcare bureaucrats would come after her. So far, her success and constant surveillance had not allowed them to do so.

Today, with Ryan gone working on a project with their pilot, Radley Baker, Meiling felt vulnerable. She needed to hear comforting words from Ryan. Meiling reached for her cell to call him, but it buzzed in her hand.

The display indicated a call from the 202 area code, Washington D.C. She answered.

"Meiling, this is Kendall Conroe. The president wanted to call you himself, but he had another important matter to attend to."

What was so important that the president wanted to talk to her personally? They had become friends over the past few months, but Meiling couldn't shake her sense of foreboding after hearing the president's Chief of Staff on the other end of the line.

"Are you still there, Meiling?"

"Yes. Why did the president want to talk to me?"

"He has repeatedly reminded you that the deep-state bureaucrats do not like your intrusion into what they consider their little fiefdoms."

"I know that they have never cooperated with our Marburg response. What are they up to now?"

"They're up to no good. That's what. The Assistant Secretary of the DHHS contacted the Colorado Medical Board (CMB) to inform them that you are practicing medicine in Colorado without a license. The DHHS wants to see you prosecuted so it can gain control of the nation's response to the Novel Marburg Virus. U.S. Code makes it a felony to practice medicine without a license in any of the fifty states."

Were they trying to convict her of a felony? It sounded like something the CCP might do. "But I didn't practice medicine. I only performed research to develop therapeutics. I did administer them to four people, but only to save their lives. They would have died. Three were Chinese citizens whom I treated while in China and over international waters. I only treated one American in the United States, my husband, Ryan Adams, and there will be no civil suit because he won't sue me. I saved his life."

“Nevertheless, there are criminal penalties for practicing medicine without a license. And they will say treating the man you married is a felony.”

“Based on my education, research, and practice at the UHK Medical School, I submitted the forms required to become licensed in Colorado.”

“But you haven’t been granted a license yet. In your case, it might seem to be a minor technicality, but practicing medicine without a license is illegal in all states. Sentences range from one to eight years in prison, depending on whether it's a misdemeanor or felony offense. Many judges will also impose fines in addition to prison sentences. Remember, Meiling, they are coming after you because you are an obstacle to their plans to run the pandemic response and profit from it.”

“What do you and the president suggest I do?”

“Well, the CMB has referred your case to the Colorado Attorney General. No doubt, they will expedite this matter, and you will probably hear from them soon. You should check with Dr. Pierce to see which lawyer he recommends because you need representation.”

“But I am working for President Warrington on the national and international pandemic responses. And I don’t have a regular medical practice. Doesn’t that carry any legal weight in the matter?”

“It should. But they will likely push this issue anyway. In the past, the CMB has warned people to cease and desist before starting prosecution. Since they view you as their enemy, they probably will not grant you that courtesy. We just wanted to let you know what was coming so you could be prepared. Let me know if you have any questions, and please, Meiling, get a good lawyer.”

Kendall ended the call.

Meiling set her cell on the table and let the reality of what was happening sink in. She had been a citizen of the

U.S. for less than three months, and the country she already loved was trying to prosecute her.

I need Ryan now.

But Ryan was with Baker, working on the Huey Cobra helicopter, configuring it with weapons to better protect the lab from physical attack. But what about legal attack—treachery from the government she had committed to serve by managing the war against the Marburg Pandemic?

Meiling lurched to grab her cell when its alarm for an incoming call startled her. She didn't recognize the number or the area code, so she opted for caution.

"Hello."

"May I speak to Meiling Chen-Adams?"

"May I ask who is calling?"

"This is Randal White, Deputy Attorney General of Colorado."

So it had already begun. As Kendall had told Meiling, "... you will probably hear from them soon." That was an understatement.

"Are you still there, Ms. Chen-Adams?"

"***Doctor*** Chen-Adams is here. What business does the Attorney General's office have with me?"

"That remains to be seen. But I wanted to give you advance notice that you will soon be served with a subpoena regarding practicing medicine without a license in the State of Colorado. Someone will be coming to your home to serve the subpoena. It must be served in person."

"My home is inside a compound containing the Bio-Safety Level 4 lab where I work. If you want to serve me with your preposterous papers, you will have to come inside."

"Don't make this any more difficult than it already is, Dr. Chen-Adams."

"So you ***do*** recognize me as a doctor?"

"As an **unlicensed** doctor."

"What about as a Ph.D. and an M.D. managing the United States response to the Novel Marburg Pandemic and working directly for President Warrington?"

"That is completely irrelevant, Ms. Chen-Adams."

"So it's ***Ms.*** Chen-Adams again. Fine. Be sure to send someone who is prepared to suit up and join Dr. Meiling Chen-Adams in the BSL-4 lab because that is where you will find me. Goodbye, Mr. White."

She hung up before he could respond.

That might keep the attorney general away for a while, but eventually, someone would serve the subpoena. And before that time, Meiling needed to find a good attorney through Robert.

She hit Dr. Robert Pierce's entry on her speed dial.

He answered on the first ring.

"This is Robert. I've been trying to reach you, but you must have been on your phone."

"I was talking to Kendall Conroe. Robert, I need your help with an important matter."

"Meiling, whatever it is, we have a higher priority matter to handle."

"But, Robert—"

"Listen, Meiling. Where our mAbs are being used in Bambari, a town in the Central African Republic, more than two hundred people who received the infusion have died in the past two days. The deep state media sharks have just discovered the deaths, and they smell blood. They are blaming you."

Chapter 2

9:30 a.m., near the Utah Test and Training Range, Hill AFB, Utah

Radley Baker turned his Huey Cobra attack helicopter to the southwest after taking off from Hill Air Force Base. Cruising at one hundred seventy-five miles per hour soon brought the Cobra over the Great Salt Lake. In another fifteen minutes, they would arrive at the Utah Test and Training Range. Colonel West had obtained permission for Baker to test the armament he had added to restore the Cobra to combat readiness.

Ryan Adams had helped them load the ammo near Rocky Mountain Metro, and then Ryan had gone to his weather station in Pierce's lab to monitor conditions for the weapons testing at the training range.

Rafer Jackson, Baker's pilot of choice for the bird, sat in front of Baker, where Rafer had both flight and weapon controls.

As much as Baker hungered to blast the targets the Range Safety Officer (RSO) set up, he realized that Rafer would likely be the pilot if the lab came under attack. Rafer needed the feel of the weapons mounted on the stub wings—the M134 Minigun and the 40 mm grenade launcher.

A call alert came in via the radio.

"I'll take the call," Baker said. "You take over the controls."

Baker answered the call.

"Cobra one, this is Adams at the weather station."

"Adams, this is Baker in Cobra one. What's up?"

"Just wanted to let you know the thunderstorms in your area won't develop until about sixteen hundred hours. You'll be long gone by then. Your visibility should be fifteen miles plus. Winds will be out of the south all afternoon. Enjoy your time at the range. Wish I could have gone with you."

"Wish you could have seen the action too. But the combat configuration of this bird only has two seats. Thanks for the info, Ryan. Cobra one out." Baker hung up the radio mic.

"Did you hear that, Rafe?"

"Yes. The weather sounds perfect for our weapon testing."

"Let's go over the target layout once more."

"Okay, Baker. Let me see if I understand it correctly."

"Shoot, Rafe."

Rafer chuckled. "I intend to. And I can't wait to see this machine gun grenade launcher shoot High Explosive Dual Purpose grenades (HEDPs) at a rate of seven per second."

"Remember, we have two target areas in a line."

"Right. Each simulates an attack force of two, twenty-five-man platoons deployed in an area the size of a football field."

"We test the grenade launcher on the first area."

"Yeah," Rafer said. "Incoming, I shoot two one-second bursts before we pass over the targets. The first burst takes the left half of the target, and the second burst takes the right half."

"The two bursts should cover the entire football-field-size area," Baker said.

"Right. Then thirty seconds ahead is an identical layout where we test the M134 Gatling gun with the same shooting pattern."

"You got it," Baker said. "But we may not hit all of the targets with the M134. Half would be enough. In a combat situation at the lab, that would probably send the others running away before we completely wiped them out."

"I've got a question," Rafer said. "How do we know how many we hit?"

"This is a low-budget firing test that West set up for us with the USAF, so we have to do the count ourselves. That keeps the cost down." Baker paused. "We'll make a second pass over both targets, hovering for a few seconds while we do an eyeball count. That will tell us all we need to know about the armament and your effectiveness in using it."

"Yeah, I guess it will." Rafer chuckled again. "With the low-character thugs we would be dealing with, they would run if they saw us take out half of their men in two seconds using the Gatling gun."

"And if they didn't run after the second pass, they would all be out of the fight."

"We can estimate the percentage close enough for government work." Rafer paused and corrected their heading a few degrees. "Five more minutes to the target. I'm checking the weapon system status one more time."

"Ryan said the wind was out of the south. Smoke will be drifting to the north. You will want to take the right half of the target on the first burst so the smoke and dust are drifting away from the area you're targeting with the second burst."

"Got it."

"Start firing at three hundred meters."

"Got it, Baker. You know, you sound like you'd rather be doing the shooting, bro."

"I won't deny it. Been shooting since I was a little kid. Gives you a sense of power ... unless somebody's shooting back at you."

"If I ever have to do this for a real attack, hopefully, I can take them all out before they can get a shot at me."

"And, Rafe, that's why we attack at one hundred fifty miles per hour."

Rafe adjusted the speed. "Here we go."

A rapid staccato of shots came from the grenade gun.

Smoke and dust exploded into the air, first on the right, then on the left of the target.

Rafer scanned the target area. "Holy smoke!"

"You got that right. But in a real attack, the guys on the ground would not think it's so holy. Get ready with the Gatling gun, Rafe. The second target is coming up."

Two more bursts sounded with the zipping noise of a powerful machine gun shooting one hundred rounds per second.

Dust kicked up on both sides of the second target, but not enough to obscure it.

"Good shooting, Rafe. Let's give it another minute for the wind to clear out the first target, then turn this bird around, and we'll see how many targets we left standing."

Two minutes later, Rafer had the Cobra hovering over the edge of the M134 Minigun targets.

"I'd say we hit at least fifty percent of the targets," Rafer said.

"And I'd say you're right. Let's move on to the grenade launcher targets."

Rafer worked the controls, and the Huey surged forward toward the next target area.

"The smoke has cleared," Baker said.

"Yeah. But I don't see any targets."

"Rafe, that's because you got them all. If we ever have to use our Cobra against an attack, it's sure death for all the attackers."

"But we can only be that effective in a surprise attack," Rafer said. "That means we need to keep our bird a secret, which means we need a way to store it out of sight."

"There's a way to do that," Baker said. "But we'll need some help from our liaison, Colonel West."

"We have thunderstorms with hail, blizzards, and high winds in Colorado. We've got to hide it, protect it, and have quick access."

"As I said, there's a way. We need to rent hangar space. We need ground-handling wheels for a Huey Cobra or a helicopter dolly big enough to handle our bird. I had a dolly back in Oregon, but it wasn't practical to move it to Colorado. However, there's another problem we need to solve."

"The ammo?" Rafer asked.

"Yeah. We need permission to store the minigun ammo and explosive RPGs in that hangar we've had our eye on, the one we would share with other birds and their pilots. That will require some help from Colonel West ... or the president."

***

Ryan locked the computer in the weather lab and headed for the apartment. Since Baker didn't need Ryan's help when the Cobra returned, he would check on Meiling.

When he entered their apartment, Meiling was sitting on the living room couch, looking as if she might cry.

"What's wrong, sweetheart?"

She stood, hurried to him, and circled him with her arms. "They are coming after me."

"Who is coming after you?"

"Everybody. The CMB told the Colorado Attorney General to charge me with multiple felonies. It is just like the president said. And they're accusing me of practicing without a license for treating you for the Nipah Virus."

"What? But that's crazy!"

"But that is not all." She paused and sniffled. "People in the Central African Republic are dying after taking our mAbs infusion."

"How many?"

"More than two hundred."

"Do we know why?"

"No, and—"

"Meiling, you're not considering going to the Central African Republic, are you? That's an unstable country with civil war more of the time than not. And you are pregnant."

"Sweetheart, I don't even have a baby bump yet. I have to go, Ryan. We cannot let our enemies, whoever they are, stop the president's plan for treating Marburg. If that were to happen, half the people on this planet would die, maybe more."

"So you need to leave immediately?"

"Yes. And we will need most of the team to track down the real killers."

"When do you plan to leave?"

"Tomorrow if at all possible."

Ryan pulled his arms from Meiling and looked at the front door. "Then I need to go back to the lab and call Ryan on the radio. He needs to be planning this trip as he's flying home from Utah. You should come with me, Meiling. He will have questions for you, and you can bet on that."

"Yes. I need to brief Ryan and then contact Robert and Ming to tell them we're going to Bambari, Central African Republic."

When Meiling and Ryan strode into the weather station, Ryan headed for the radio and fired it up.

"Adams at the weather station calling Cobra one."

"Adams, this is Cobra one. What's up?"

"Some really nasty stuff has hit the fan. The upshot of it all is that most of our team is going to the Central African Republic, and you're flying us there."

"Adams, you're kidding me, right?"

"No, bro. People are dying in droves over there after receiving our mAbs. We've got to go to the Central African Republic."

"When is this trip supposed to happen?"

"Cobra one, I'll let Meiling brief you on the details, but we leave tomorrow."

"So you really ***are*** kidding me."

"Cobra one, this is Meiling. You need to work up a flight plan for the most direct route to Bambari, Central African Republic. And we ***do*** leave tomorrow. If not, a lot more people could die."

Chapter 3

6:40 p.m., the conference room in Pierce's lab

Meiling sat beside Ryan in the conference room with her cell in her ear.

She listened as Jeff Langstrom, the CEO of MABS International, explained his company's procedures for releasing a shipment of mAbs.

"So you keep a sample from each shipment?"

"Yes, Meiling. Without fail."

"I need you to send to Robert's lab 0.1 milliliters from your sample from the shipment that went to Bambari, Central African Republic. Our lab will analyze it for any possible impurities or additives. You should do the same, and then we'll compare notes."

"We will send the sample via courier first thing tomorrow morning."

"Great. Dr. Li and Dr. Ren will do the analysis at our lab. The rest of us will fly to Bambari tomorrow to work backward from that end. We must find what made these people sick and trace it to its source."

They ended the call just as Robert entered the conference room.

"I'm all packed and ready to go. Was that Langstrom you were talking to?"

"Yes," Meiling said. "He's sending us a sample from the batch that went to the Regional Hospital at Bambari."

"Lee and Jinghua will be here to analyze it. He has taken Jinghua under his wing like she was his daughter. They work well together."

"How is Jinghua with that relationship?" Ryan said.

Robert chuckled. "Since all the changes we've seen in Lee, Jinghua seems to enjoy working with him. Speak of the devil."

Lee and Jinghua walked into the room and sat down, leaving the chair beside Robert empty.

Ming came in shortly after the two. She squeezed Robert's shoulder and then sat beside him.

Baker trudged in carrying a bag of potato chips from the vending machine and a can of Pepsi. "Sorry, Meiling. You caused me to miss my dinner, so you get the privilege of hearing me crunch on potato chips."

"Permission granted as long as you do not pop your shoulders. That gives me the creeps."

"Uh, I didn't ask permission. But I do want to introduce a new member of our team."

"Do you mean Rafer?" Ryan asked.

"No. I mean pilot Buck McKinney."

Meiling saw Ryan and Robert giving Baker ***the look.***

Robert opened his mouth, but Ryan beat him to the words. "This is a sensitive mission, Baker. Who is Buck McKinney, and why do we need him?"

"On our last excursion to Wuhan land, I got too tired to be entrusted with you and our plane's safety. This little jaunt to Bambari is a thirteen-hour flight plus a little stop time in Casablanca to refuel. Buck has almost a thousand hours on Gulfstreams, including five hundred hours on G550s. He's a friend from Oregon and a vet I served with. Any other questions?"

"Can he make it to the airport by 7:00 a.m. tomorrow?" Meiling asked.

Baker met her gaze and crunched extra loudly on a handful of chips. "He'll be there, and he'll fit in just fine. In fact, he kind of reminds me of me."

"Thanks for the warning," Meiling said, sensing she was almost smiling. But their current circumstances did not give her much to smile about.

"It sounds like Baker has the flight planned. In the morning, a courier will arrive with a mAbs sample from MABS International. It is from the batch that went to the Bambari Regional Hospital. Lee and Jinghua will remain here to run the lab and analyze the sample for any impurities or additives that could account for the deaths in Bambari. Lee, Robert, and I are leaving you in charge of the lab with Jinghua second in command.

"Here is what the rest of us must do in Bambari. We must conduct two parallel investigations. One will be to find the point at which something happened to the mAbs to cause the deaths and then to determine who or what caused it. The second investigation examines those those who died after getting the mAbs and to determine what killed them and how it accomplished that.

"Robert, since you have the most experience treating patients and with autopsies, will you handle that part of the examination?"

"Yes. Ming can help me, especially if we have blood or tissue samples to analyze."

"Great." Meiling turned to Baker, who had just stuffed his mouth with potato chips. "Baker, you and Mr. McKinney—"

"Don't call him that, Meiling, if you want to stay on his good side. He's just Buck."

"Okay. You and Buck can note any place from the airport to the clinic or the hospital where someone could have contaminated the mAbs. Find out who was there on the day of delivery and ask if they saw anything suspicious.

"Ryan and I will follow the chain of custody of the mAbs from the delivery points outside of the clinic and the hospital to where the healthcare workers administered the infusions. Any questions?"

"I've got a question," Baker said. "How long is this investigation going to take?"

Meiling blew out a sharp sigh. "As long as it takes us to identify the culprit or culprits. Realistically, if we cannot do that in three days, we probably will not solve the mystery. But we need answers ASAP, so we sleep on the plane and hit the ground running in Bambari."

Baker set his chips down on the table and stood. "Apologies in advance for my assertions, Meiling, but here's the way I see it. If you all haven't heard, the Colorado Attorney General is trying to prosecute Meiling for practicing without a license, and now we have this apparent deadly failure with Meiling's mAbs. I think the bureaucrats and big pharmaceutical companies are trying to eliminate Meiling so they can take over handling the nation's Marburg Virus response. If they can do that now, there's still time for them to make a lot of money on this pandemic like they did on the COVID pandemic a few years ago."

Ryan swiveled his chair toward Baker. "My thoughts exactly. And if we're right, we need to send those responsible to prison because I believe we will find that the deaths in Bambari are murder."

"Yes, murder," Baker said. "That's why we could be in danger on this mission. And because people's friends and family members have died from Meiling's mAbs, we could arrive and find a hostile audience. After this meeting, I will touch bases with Colonel West about security issues." Ryan, bring your Sig Sauer, and I'll bring my M4 and a handgun."

Meiling stood. "Baker is right. While we are in Bambari, be vigilant. If there has been murder, the murderers will want to ensure we do not identify them. They have already killed over two hundred men, women, and children in

Bambari and may be attempting to cause deaths in other places. They are desperate and will not hesitate to kill us."

Chapter 4

8:00 p.m., secure conference room, Phisher Pharmaceuticals Headquarters, East Manhattan

Phisher Pharmaceuticals CEO, Abe Borland, scanned the faces around the large conference table—Dr. Wally Gantz from Mercer Medical, CDC Chief Operating Officer Dr. Marshall McDowell, Dr. Yanyi Shi, Deputy Director General of the Wuhan Institute of Virology and the only woman in this group, and General Liu Kuo of the People's Liberation Army (PLA).

Abe stood. "Gentlemen and Dr. Shi, I called this meeting because there is still a window of opportunity for Phisher and Mercer to become the preferred providers for the Novel Marburg Virus treatment. But we must deal expeditiously with Meiling Chen-Adams if we are to replace her and Dr. Pierce as President Warrington's choice for treating the virus. After Dr. Chen-Adams's work progress caused the CCP to rush the Marburg release, which Dr. Chen-Adams then countered with her mAbs and killer protein, we must vilify her until the president no longer trusts her."

"Abe," Wally Gantz stood. "We must tread softly in any attempt to, as you say, 'vilify' Meiling Chen-Adams, or we may be the ones who are vilified. How do you plan to turn Chen-Adams from rising star to fallen angel?"

"The wheels are already in motion to accomplish that, Wally. As we speak, felony charges are already being brought against Chen-Adams in the state of Colorado. In addition, people are dying after their infusions with her mAbs in the Central African Republic."

General Liu Kuo of the People's Liberation Army stood. "Did you know, Mr. Borland, that as we speak, Meiling Chen-Adams is planning a trip to Bambari to investigate the deaths?"

"General Kuo, how do you know this?"

"I have intelligence sources that assure me this trip is being planned for the immediate future, perhaps tomorrow."

Abe swore and then took a deep breath to control himself. He was the person in charge, and no one sitting around this table should doubt that or his ability to bring Meiling Chen-Adams to disfavor in the eyes of the president.

"Rest assured that no one will ever discover what happened to Chen-Adams's mAbs that is causing death among those Africans. And suppose Meiling were never to return from her African boondoggle designed to dupe the American people into using her infusion."

Wally sat down. "Remember my advice, Abe. Tread softly. One mistake, and we will never get to use our mRNA Marburg vaccines in this pandemic. That would set back our plan with the World Economic Council several years."

"Yes," General Kuo said. "And perhaps the PLA and the CCP would have to take over this entire effort at resetting the world's economy and balance of power."

"Excuse me, General Kuo," Abe said. "What do you mean by 'take over this entire effort'?"

"I mean a more forceful approach but one that still conceals our role in this effort. If these charges and the apparent failure of the mAbs in Central Africa do not give us the results we need, we must take out Pierce's entire lab and all the researchers who work there. Simultaneously, we must destroy the facilities of MABS International and ProtSyn, the manufacturer of the killer protein."

"General Kuo, how in heaven's name would you do that without drawing attention to us?" Wally said.

"The PLA has resources deep within the FBI and the CIA. We also have our police stations in New York City and Los Angeles. We have enough men to stage faux terrorist attacks to destroy facilities at all three locations and ensure the key people do not survive."

"Who would you blame the attacks on?" Abe said.

"The radical population control group, Global Threat Initiative (GTI). They would gladly do this if they had the resources to ***pull it off***, as you Americans say."

Wally straightened in his chair. "Where would you get the weaponry and munitions for such an attack?"

General Kuo gave them a twisted smile. "North Korea and Iran have already provided them."

Chapter 5

7:45 a.m. the next morning, Rocky Mountain Metro

Meiling scurried into the airport restroom, lunged toward a stall, and lost her breakfast. Her morning sickness had returned with a vengeance after subsiding for a week.

How could she function effectively as leader of the investigative team from Dr. Pierce's lab when her stomach writhed in agony and threatened to eject anything she put into it? She had the duration of a fourteen-hour flight to answer that question.

Fifteen minutes later, with a quivering stomach, she settled into a reclining seat on Baker's Gulfstream.

Ryan sat beside her and gave her a sympathetic glance. He moved a hand toward her stomach.

"Don't, sweetheart—unless you want the rest of my breakfast omelet in your lap."

"Meiling, how could such a blessing be—"

"If you think it's a blessing, you take it, Ryan. After all, this ***is*** your fault."

"***Fault?*** That's not so. Actually, it was Eve's fault because—"

"I am in no mood for an apologetical treatise. Just be still, do not touch my stomach, and do not talk about food."

Robert and Ming sat directly across the aisle from Meiling and Ryan and watched the verbal altercation with great interest; at least, that was what Ming's eyes said.

Meiling met Ming's gaze. "Take notes, Ming. Your turn is next."

"But Robert has not asked—"

"Exactly," Meiling said. "Because he is a coward."

Robert pulled his head back like he had been struck.

Ryan took Meiling's hand. "You're really in a rotten mood this morning."

"I'm sorry. It feels like I have eaten something rotten."

"Just don't let it come out through your disposition."

She opened her mouth to reply, but Baker emerged from the cockpit and entered the cabin.

A taller man, almost as muscular as Baker, followed him into the cabin. The man's shaggy blonde hair hung in curls on an intelligent-looking brow that crowned bright blue eyes.

"I'd like your attention," Baker said. "This is Buck McKinney, your co-pilot, and our new team member."

Baker introduced the team to Buck.

The diversion seemed to settle Meiling's roiling stomach.

"Listen up," Baker said. "We'll take off shortly. We'll stop in Casablanca for fuel in nine and a half hours, then four more hours to Bambari."

"That's right," Buck said. "I know y'all just got up, but by the time we get to the hospital in Bambari, it's going to be about 6:30 a.m. local time. That's bedtime in Colorado. And from what Baker told me, y'all won't get much sleep then, so get as much as you can on this flight."

Baker and Buck turned and entered the cockpit.

Buck had a charming southern accent. Meiling had heard the slow drawl only a few times since she came to the United States.

Meiling lowered her voice. "I wonder what Jinghua will think about that accent."

Ryan shook his head. "Let it be, Meiling. *Que sera sera.*"

"Whatever that means. I am suddenly exhausted, Ryan."

The whine of the idling jet engine turned to a low rumble, and the Gulfstream rolled forward toward the end of the runway.

Ryan's arm curled around her shoulders, pulling her head against his chest.

Meiling loosened her seatbelt a bit and snuggled into a comfortable position against her husband.

Her stomach had stopped churning, so she took Buck's advice and soon drifted off.

***

5:30 a.m. local time, 51,000 feet over Western Africa

The Gulfstream had landed at Casablanca to refuel a little after midnight. They now flew in what Ryan called the lower stratosphere over halfway from Casablanca to Bambari.

Meiling watched the sun pop up above the horizon ahead. A new day had begun, a day that could bring failure or fortune. Considering the portentous events ahead, there was no way she could sleep.

Perhaps it was time for a final team meeting before they landed.

First, she would have to loosen Ryan's hold on her. Though he was asleep, his arm around Meiling's shoulders held her in a firm grip.

"Ryan, I need to get up."

"Are we there yet?" His eyes popped open, and he gave her a sleepy-eyed grin.

"I think we are an hour out, so I'm going to tell Baker we are having a team meeting to ensure we are all ready to begin our tasks after landing."

Ryan moved his arm, and Meiling unbuckled the seat belt she had worn loosely for the past three hours.

She approached the cockpit door and stuck her head inside. "Baker, Buck, we are going to have a final team meeting to ensure we are all in sync and ready to go after we land in Bambari."

Baker looked at Buck seated beside him. "Take over, Buck. You can put the bird on autopilot when the meeting starts and stand in the doorway."

"I guess technically that is remaining in the cockpit," Buck said.

"There's probably nothing over Africa at fifty-one thousand feet except for a few big CBs and us. And the system's as solid as a rock."

"Aye, aye, captain. See you in a couple of minutes."

Meiling took her seat beside Ryan.

Baker walked into the cabin and joined them. Buck soon appeared in the cockpit doorway.

Ming glanced at Robert and slipped her hand from his. "We are ready, Meiling."

The first thing she needed to remind them of was the travel advisory. "We are not heading into a nice, peaceful African nation. Our state department says, 'Do not travel to the Central African Republic (CAR) due to the Embassy in Bangui's limited capacity to provide support to U.S. citizens and due to crime, civil unrest, and kidnapping'.

"With that in mind, we should never go anywhere alone. Always go in at least twos. And at least one of us in each couple will be carrying, except Robert and Ming. The hospital will not allow guns inside the patient's rooms or the morgue. Ryan, we must check with our escort if we need to enter those areas. I will introduce you as my personal bodyguard, protecting me at our government's request. Maybe that will suffice.

"Also, remember that the hospital and perhaps other facilities will have armed government guards. Do not challenge them. Comply with their requests. And be aware that you may encounter Muslim rebel forces, Christian self-defense forces, or criminals.

"Note any reluctance to answer your questions. That could be a sign of a coverup. Remember, we are looking for places where the mAbs shipments could have been compromised while being moved from the airport to the hospital. Robert and Ming will also determine what killed more than two hundred people. If the citizens blame the United States or me, that could also place us in danger.

"In the evening, we shall gather at 7:00 p.m. at the hotel, where four adjacent rooms are reserved. It is only a few blocks from the hospital. If you will be late or run into trouble, use your sat phone to notify me or Robert if I'm not available.

"We are arriving shortly after the beginning of the rainy season. It can be hot and humid, so stay hydrated and only drink bottled water. Any questions?"

"Yeah," Baker said. "If we were to run into trouble and have to shoot someone to save our lives, what then?"

"Just make sure the person you shoot is someone the government would want to be shot. The U.S. Embassy in Bangui is two hundred miles away and cannot provide consular services at this time. So, if we get into trouble, we are on our own. Of course, we can call Colonel West, but his response may take a while. So, let's pray we do not have to do that."

"I contacted the hospital," Robert said. "They were accommodating and seemed to look forward to our arrival. I think they're overwhelmed with what is happening and expect us to fix things. I pray we can do that."

"That is my prayer, too," Meiling said. "Because if we cannot, we could have trouble both here in Bambari and at home. And the FDA, the CDC, and the pharmaceutical companies would be out for blood … our blood."

Chapter 6

Bambari, Central African Republic

Meiling looked out a window of the Gulfstream and could see one side of the rapidly approaching dirt runway. "I hope Baker knows what he's doing. That runway is dirt, and it doesn't look very long."

Ryan chuckled. "Don't worry. He told me a story about stealing a military transport and setting it down on a runway half as long as the Bambari Airport. He overloaded it with people and took off."

Meiling turned her head toward Ryan. "Seriously? And you believed him? Even the part about stealing a military plane?"

"Some of his friends from Redmond were there. They vouched for him, though they thought he was crazy at the time."

She would trust Baker to get them down and back out of here when they completed their mission. After all, it was his plane, and he said it was worth twenty-five million dollars.

The plane set down softly, and the dirt runway was surprisingly smooth as the plane rolled down it.

After slowing to a taxi, Baker turned the Gulfstream toward a dingy yellow building with *Aerodrome De Bambari* painted on it.

The facts she had gleaned from the Internet last night now merged with the reality Meiling could see. The terminal had not been built for passengers, only to handle the needs of pilots flying in and out of this little airport four miles out of town. This was an impoverished area in a poor nation. Had that played a role in the deaths of more than two hundred people? She would reserve judgment until they had completed their investigation.

After Baker parked his plane, he carried a duffle bag into the cabin and prepared to open the door. "Based on what I've seen so far, I need to inquire about extra security for my bird. Buck agrees with me."

"With all the instability in the Central African Republic over the past few years, that's a good idea," Ryan said. "There are U.N. peacekeeping forces here. Maybe they will help if we tell them we're from the U.S."

After the steps lowered to the ground, Robert moved to the doorway. "I'll go inside and call a taxi for Meiling and Ryan, and Ming and me."

"I'll get your bag, Robert," Ming said.

"Buck and I need to run around a bit checking with folks from the airport to town. We think a guy here runs something like Rent-A-Wreck, so we'll get our car and meet you at noon at the hotel," Baker said. "Ryan, you've got the only gun in your group. Keep a sharp eye out for anyone up to no good."

"We will see you at noon," Meiling said.

After Ryan nodded, Baker and Buck headed down the steps, each carrying a duffle bag.

An hour later, Meiling, Ryan, Robert, and Ming sat stuffed into an old car that served as a taxi.

In another ten minutes, the taxi pulled up to a long, single-story yellow and gray building that reminded Meiling of the airport terminal building—just the bare necessities.

Meiling got out of the taxi and surveyed the hotel and its surroundings. Except for a sparse sprinkling of plants that desperately needed water, the building was unadorned and sitting on the reddish soil of Bambari.

Please, God, no bugs or rats. I know these people are

poor, but I cannot do my job to help them if bugs are—"

Ryan nudged her from behind. "We need to get checked in and then get to the hospital. I know what you're thinking, but I'll keep the bugs away."

"And how pray tell, will you do that, Mr. Adams?"

"Off. It contains Deet. It smells a bit, but it will keep flies, mosquitos, and fleas away."

"What about rats?"

"You don't want them close enough to you to smell the Off. I've got my Sig Sauer." He grinned.

"If you shoot that in our room, we might start a war. From what I read, this country may have calmed down a bit after the last revolution, but it is still simmering like it is about to boil."

"Then I sure don't want to apply any heat to it."

"Clever, sweetheart. But we need to catch up with Robert and Ming to get checked in at the office."

"Go ahead. I'll grab Baker's and Buck's duffle bags to put them in their room." He gave Meiling a crooked smile. "You know, we could have rented three rooms instead of four if we had two men's rooms and a ladies' room."

Pictures of her and Ming assaulted by fleas and spiders scrolled across the screen of Meiling's mind. "That is not going to happen, Ryan. You will protect me, or I will not sleep." She scanned the lobby area and the hotel desk.

I might not sleep anyway.

As Meiling and Ryan approached the desk, Robert spoke to the hotel manager in French.

In a few moments, with keys in his hand, Robert turned to Meiling and Ryan. "I put this on my card. We're going to submit our expenses to Colonel West. One card will be easier to deal with."

"Then we should put our bags in our rooms and hurry to the hospital," Meiling said.

Five minutes later, all four stood outside of the motel office.

Ryan pointed to the north. "This way. It's only a couple of country blocks to the hospital."

"We have three hours until lunch," Meiling said. "Let us see what we can accomplish."

They strode toward the street that would take them to the hospital.

"Ming, what did you think of your room?" Meiling said.

"It will do, hopefully for only one night, if we can solve this mystery today. But it did have a light coating of red dust."

Meiling nodded. "With almost no landscaping in the town, everything in Bambari has a coating of red dust."

"Let's hurry," Ryan said. "If the wind picks up a little more, ***we*** will be coated in red dust too."

Five minutes later, they weaved between buildings and hut-like shelters until they found what appeared to be the administration building.

"Let's introduce ourselves," Robert said. "That will tell us a lot about the cooperation we will get."

When Robert introduced himself, an administrator and a nursing supervisor smiled and appeared helpful. But when Robert introduced Meiling, the smiles ended, and the look on their faces turned to contempt.

Meiling wanted to tell them she understood their feelings, but it was best to solve the mystery and then convince them of the truth about what had happened at the Bambari hospital.

She also wanted to give them the thirty doses of her killer protein that she had packed in her duffle bag, but the look on the nurse's and administrator's faces said they did not trust her and would likely throw them in the biological hazard container. The killer protein would have to wait.

The nurse left the desk, and Robert turned to Meiling and Ryan. “They sent for someone to take us to the morgue. There are five bodies still here after the rash of deaths.”

“Will you ask them if they can provide any personal protection equipment for us? Maybe they will do so for you and Ming, but I do not know about me.”

“So, you caught that reaction too. Don’t worry, Meiling. They will quickly change their minds about you when we all learn the truth about what happened here.”

The man at the desk stood. “Were you asking about PPE?”

“Yes,” Robert said as he turned toward the man. “Do you have equipment for us?”

The man nodded. “We have N95 masks and gloves.”

“That should work for us. All four of us have immunity from Novel Marburg.”

“I see that you did not give your lives for it.” The man’s remark came dripping with sarcasm.

“No,” Meiling said. “And no one here should have died either. I will take full responsibility for those deaths until the truth is discovered. But so that you know—no one has died from the infusions anywhere else in the world.”

The administrator’s expression morphed from disdain to curiosity.

Meiling continued. “Do you have any empty or full infusion bags from the batches of mAbs that the U.S. State Department delivered?”

“Yes. We have at least one partially filled bag from each batch. When Nurse Adamu returns, she can take you to the coolers where we stored the infusions.”

“Thank you.”

The nurse returned with a short, stocky man in scrubs following her. She stopped near Ming and Robert. “This is Nzinga, the keeper of our morgue. He will show you the way to the morgue and the bodies you wish to examine.”

"I hope you're ready for this, Ming," Robert said as he hooked her arm. "I'm assuming they died from Marburg, so it won't be pleasant."

"Robert, I am an M.D. We see a lot of unpleasant things in our training and practice."

Robert motioned ahead. "Show us the way, Nzinga."

Meiling called out to Robert and Ming. "See you at the hospital office at about five until noon." She turned to the head nurse. "Nurse Adamu, what is your most powerful microscope at the hospital?"

The nurse folded her arms across her chest. "Now that the violence has been brought under control, we have purchased a used electron microscope."

"May we use it to examine the plasma cells we collect?"

"What are you looking for in plasma cells?"

Should she say at this point? "We are looking to see what the state of the mAbs was in the patients who died and then match the findings to the batch of mAbs."

"What do you expect to see?"

"The truth. We need to know the truth, whatever it turns out to be. We can only fix what is broken; the truth will tell us what that is."

The nurse opened her mouth to speak, then closed it again.

"Nurse Adamu, the only thing we can do to help the families of those who died is to honor those who died by acknowledging what killed them." Meiling wanted to say more, but it would not be appropriate at this juncture.

The pensive expression on the nurse's face said that perhaps Meiling was winning over a valuable partner.

Nurse Adamu motioned toward a side door. "Follow me. I will show you the mAbs we have preserved and the lab with the microscope."

"Are the bags labeled with the batch that they came from?"

“What do you—I mean, yes, they are labeled.”

The nurse led Meiling and Ryan into a room that housed a refrigeration unit. But on a long table in front of the unit, a row of what looked like lab specimens were neatly lined up.

Nurse Adamu left.

Meiling hurried to the table and read the labels by each specimen. These were specimens of the mAbs labeled by batch. Each sample was tagged with a message that read, dehydrated and ready for final drying.

“Nice of her to tell us.”

“To tell us what?” Ryan stepped beside her and scanned the table.

Ryan stepped back and leaned against the wall. “To tell us what, Meiling?”

“That they had already prepared the specimens for viewing on the electron microscope. Well, all but the final dehydration and mounting on the stub.”

“I don’t think the nurse or the administrator like you, Meiling. I hope the hostility we saw in the office is the only hostility we encounter on this trip. I’ve got my gun, but …”

“Ryan, until we know what killed more than two hundred people here in this hospital, we do not know what we might encounter. Now, let me take some samples to that lab she pointed out on the way here. With a little luck, we will be looking at lymphocytes in less than thirty minutes. I saw at least one light microscope in that lab. I can use a light scope to speed up this process.”

Forty-five minutes later, Meiling had the third sample from the third mAbs batch in the microscope.

“Meiling, fifteen minutes ago, you said you would tell me what you are seeing.”

“I will, sweetheart. Just let me look at the third sample for a few minutes. If it matches the other two, I think we have found the problem.”

"Nothing like keeping a guy in suspense. What kind of problem are we talking about?"

"Let me concentrate on getting this sample scanned. Then, if my findings are consistent with what Robert and Ming find, we have a lot to talk about during lunch."

"You're not gonna tell me about your findings, are you?"

"The longer you distract me, the longer it will be before I can tell you."

Ryan plopped into a plastic lawn chair against the wall and folded his arms.

When the scan was completed, and she looked at the results, it confirmed Meiling's suspicions.

She removed her sample and prepared to shut down the microscope.

"Now, are you going to tell me?"

'This does not tell me how, when, or where it happened, but it does tell me ***what*** happened."

"Do you enjoy doing this to me, Meiling? So what happened?"

"I'm sorry, sweetheart. I was deep in thought."

"Obviously not about me. I'll forgive you if you'll just tell me what the heck happened to our mAbs."

"Ryan, remember what the pastor who married us said. Using minced expletives is almost as bad as—"

"If you don't tell me right now what happened to the mAbs, I won't mince anything."

"Relax, Ryan. I am going to tell you." She paused.

"Just tell me what you—"

"They were cooked."

"What?"

"The only time I've ever seen lymphocytes look like those samples is when they had been heated. We call it cooking. It kills their ability to do anything except wait to be disposed of by the body they are in."

“But the State Department Gulfstreams all had cooling systems onboard to store the mAbs.”

“I know. But before we jump to any further conclusions, we should hear what Robert and Ming found from the bodies in the morgue. I am glad they took that assignment. It could not have been pleasant.”

“This is all starting to make sense, Meiling.”

“Hold your conspiracy theories until we hear from Robert and Ming. If their findings support your theory, you can fire away.”

“I’m hungry. What time is it?”

She pulled out her cell and checked the display. “It’s eleven thirty. We now know enough to call my work here complete. I will clean up my mess in the lab, and then we can walk back to the office to meet Robert and Ming.”

When Meiling and Ryan arrived at the hospital office, Robert and Ming stood outside the entrance.

Ryan approached Robert. “I see someone else got hungry too.”

Ming shook her head. “Robert and I are not hungry.”

“I am. Speak for yourself, Ming.”

Ming’s beautiful face contorted into an unpleasant caricature of itself. “Robert, how can you think about food after looking at what Marburg does to the human body?”

“Robert.” Meiling drew Robert’s gaze. “Did you complete your examinations?”

“Yes. I believe we obtained all the information we need to explain how these people died and to form a strong hypothesis as to what caused the deaths.”

“I see,” Meiling said. “Let’s hold our findings until we all can present and discuss them with the whole team. We need to see the whole picture before drawing firm conclusions, and we cannot afford to jump to a wrong conclusion.”

"Then let's go back to the hotel," Ryan said. "We're supposed to meet Baker and Buck there at noon. It's ten 'til noon now."

When the four reached the hotel, Baker's and Buck's Rent-A-Wreck car, an old Toyota sedan, was parked in front of their room, and the two sat on a fender in a spot partially shaded by a scrubby tree.

Baker slid off the fender. "My map says the closest restaurant is about three blocks beyond the hospital. We're hungry. Let's go eat."

"What's the name of this place," Robert asked.

"The Patisserie. Does that mean something like a bakery?"

"Yes. It means a place that makes pastries. And that's why it might not be the best place for lunch."

"Back home, bakeries usually had a deli inside. Let's try it. We'd have to drive to the other restaurants."

The Patisserie sat on a corner at the center of Bambari.

The team of six crossed the dusty main street with very little traffic and entered the restaurant.

Robert surveyed the large assortment of baked goods displayed in the glass cases under the counter. "I'm not sure we can find lunch here."

"But look at all stuff in those glass cases under the counter," Baker said. "It doesn't all look like dessert.

"Some bread and a bottle of water from their cooler, and I'm good to go," Buck said.

"Okay. Grab what you want, and I'll put it all on my card," Robert said.

The Patisserie was crowded inside, so Meiling looked for a place to sit with more privacy. "We can sit at the big table out on the veranda. It's shaded and will be quieter out there."

Five minutes later, all six were seated around the table on the veranda. The veranda was a long, covered porch supported by three large pillars painted to match the red dirt of Bambari. Their table looked out onto the main street that circled the front of the restaurant at the center of the town.

"What did you and Buck find out about the delivery?" Ryan asked.

"Nothing out of the ordinary," Baker said. "But there was a big folderol to celebrate the arrival of an American treatment that was going to save their people."

Meiling sighed. "That explains the hospital staff's reaction when introduced to me." She paused. "Shall we share what we found and see what conclusions we can draw?"

Robert took a drink and set his water bottle on the table. "Ming and I determined that the victims all died a typical, gruesome Marburg death. It was as if they had never been treated."

"And that corresponds with what I saw using the hospital's electron microscope. Each sample of mAbs from three different batches had been cooked."

"Cooked?" Baker's eyebrows rose.

"They heated the mAbs sometime before it was delivered, and that destroyed the antibodies," Robert said.

"And thus it was 'as if they had never been treated'." Baker blew out a blast of frustration.

"It appears that we know ***what*** was done," Ryan said. "But who did it and why?" He scanned the faces around the table.

"We need to keep what happened here in perspective," Meiling said. "A few years ago, rebels and mercenaries took the town of Bambari. The rebels targeted civilians. Roads in the area were mined—it took a heavy toll on the people here.

"The war destroyed most of the agricultural production. Eighty percent of the people in this republic live below the poverty level. Many are still starving. That is why the U.N.

World Food Program is here. This is the poorest nation in Africa."

"Maybe that's why the Marburg murderers picked it to kill people," Ming said. "They thought nobody would care. Or if they did care, they would be too poor and powerless to do anything about it."

"You're probably right, Ming," Meiling said. "We must stop the killing of sick people and identify those responsible. The people here have so much stacked against them in this life. They do not need any more grief."

"The people in Bambari are so far removed from our world that I cannot see them getting involved in power struggles with the U.S. or its government," Ming said. "They are only concerned with having enough food and getting treatment for their families if they get sick."

"Yes," Ryan said. "But they might take money for carrying out a task that someone else puts them up to."

Meiling laid her hand on Ryan's shoulder. "Possibly, but in that case, the person we want is the one who put them up to the task."

"And everything points back to the U.S. delivery to Bambari and the State Department that handled it," Ryan said.

Robert swallowed the last bite of his foot-long piece of bread stuffed with things Meiling could not identify. "And this is what it appears happened. Someone, most likely during shipping, applied forced degradation conditions to the mAbs. The culprit cooked them and probably added a base to raise the pH."

"I think you are right, Robert," Meiling said. "I detected a higher-than-normal pH in the mAbs from the infusion bags the hospital saved for us."

Robert blasted out a sharp sigh. "The heat and pH change would cause protein degradation in a short amount of time—on the order of the time it takes to fly a shipment from Minneapolis to Bambari. The people in Bambari infected with Novel Marburg Virus were given mAbs that could not have worked. Ming and I observed the result. They died a terrible Marburg death as if they had never been treated."

"That's horrible," Meiling said. "It's cruel. It's evil beyond belief. Who would go so far just to remove me from my advisory role with President Warrington?"

Ryan gave her a sardonic smile. "How much time do you have, Meiling? I can think of a long list of people. As Robert hinted, someone in the State Department likely did the demonic deed, but the orders to do it could have come from the FDA, CDC, DHHS, any leftist government bureaucrat, or the pharmaceutical companies. If they knew in advance about the coming Marburg Pandemic, there was a lot of money to be made, especially through a vaccine ... until ***you*** stole the show."

"You mean through another ***fake*** vaccine?" Baker said. "The kind they foisted on us for COVID-19?"

"That toxic spike protein was what made the mRNA vaccines so dangerous," Robert said. "It wreaked havoc with several organs, especially the heart and the rest of the circulatory system. And it crossed the blood-brain barrier, causing strokes and other brain issues, including prion diseases like Creutzfeldt-Jakob disease, ALS, and Parkinson's. With the Novel Marburg Virus, who knows what proteins they picked for the vaccine to produce antibodies? I doubt if they could have picked anything worse than the spike protein. But because of the mRNA approach, I doubt it would have been much better."

"Either the pharmaceutical companies had no clue what they were doing by letting their mRNA carrying a toxic protein run loose in the human body, or they just did not care," Meiling said. "The mRNA is busy replicating, so it never gets cleaned up quickly. That's why I only use the mRNA approach for a killer protein and only when it is absolutely required to save a life. Then I purge it from the patient's body with several infusions to ensure no mRNA is left after it completes its job."

"But we are getting off track here," Robert said. "We know what happened to our mAbs. Now we need a strategy to identify the guilty parties, both the person who did it and the one who gave the order to cripple our mAbs."

Meiling surveyed the faces around the table. "I say that we rule out MABS International. Their process control would not allow them to cook the shipment before loading it onto a government plane."

"Agreed," Robert said. "Let's focus on the shipment of the mAbs from Minneapolis to Bambari. Who had the opportunity to heat the shipment, and when could they have done it?"

Baker pointed at some imaginary target with his empty water bottle. "I know for a fact that the State Department Gulfstream landed at Casablanca to refuel. We need to check that flight and see how long it took that pilot to make it to Bambari. Maybe they spent some time at Casablanca."

"How could someone heat the entire shipment of mAbs, and how long would it have taken?" Robert said.

"It was not a big shipment," Meiling said. "MABS International ships using BFS advanced 100-milliliter bottles packed in boxes."

"Is a box of bottles about the size of a five-gallon bucket?" Baker asked.

"The bucket might hold ten boxes of bottles," Meiling said.

"What if they opened the boxes and dumped the bottles into five-gallon buckets?"

What was Baker getting at? "Baker, why are you asking that?"

"Because you can buy off-the-shelf warming blankets made to fit five-gallon buckets."

Meiling shrugged. "I am not sure. Maybe thirty boxes would fill a bucket."

"How many boxes went to Bambari, Meiling?"

Meiling quickly did the math. "We sent enough to treat about half of the population of Bambari—three hundred boxes, so about ten five-gallon buckets."

So ten heating blankets.

"If the plane stopped before leaving the Continental U.S., they could have packed the vials in buckets, wrapped them in heating blankets set at 160 degrees, cooked them all the way to Casablanca, then repacked the vials."

"That may not be exactly how they did it," Meiling said. "But it shows that it is feasible to cook our mAbs during the flight with a stop at each end of the cooking cycle."

Ryan looked across the table at Baker. "Could the G550's electrical system simultaneously handle ten heating blankets?"

"No problem," Baker said.

"So, who would have known about this heating of the mAbs?" Ryan asked.

"Well, the pilot and co-pilot, for sure," Buck said.

"The person who told them what to do and the person with authority to order it," Meiling said.

Robert stroked his beard a few times. "We should ask the president to send a hand-picked law-enforcement team to arrest the pilot and co-pilot and then charge them with over two hundred murders. One of them would probably go for a plea deal and would incriminate the people who masterminded and ordered this crime."

"This is a nightmare," Ming said. "This could be repeated at any time. To stop it in the future, we would need trusted security on each flight to guard the shipment to its destination."

"I just had another thought," Meiling said. "The State Department has no expertise in mAbs. They would not know that heat could destroy the antibodies. But the pharmaceutical companies would know, and they would be the primary beneficiaries of this murderous attempt to remove our lab from overseeing the president's Marburg response."

Ryan leaned back in his chair and grinned. "Using the pilots to flush them out may be the best way to nail the big pharma crooks."

A white pickup with UN painted on its door skidded around the corner in front of The Patisserie and then slowed.

The three men in the back of the pickup stared at them.

Meiling was sure they were staring at her.

The men raised automatic rifles.

Chapter 7

Ryan reached for Meiling when the white truck appeared from around the corner.

That tingling sensation a person gets when something isn't right, possibly threatening, ran from his neck down his spine.

The logo on the door said UN, but the letters were not nicely stenciled. They were sloppily hand-painted.

His gaze went to the men in the back dressed in camouflage clothing and holding what appeared to be AK-47s now swinging upward in Meiling's direction.

"Attack! Take cover!" Ryan hooked an arm around Meiling and shoved her against the back side of a large pillar supporting the roof of the veranda.

The staccato belching of three automatic rifles turned the quiet street into cacophony and chaos.

On Ryan's left, Robert jerked Ming to the veranda floor and sheltered behind a two-foot-high concrete fence.

Baker and Buck dove for the concrete fence on Ryan's right.

The shots continued for several seconds.

The large front window of The Patisserie exploded, sending glass shards clattering across the floor.

The people inside screamed.

Ryan kept Meiling pressed hard against the pillar and slid her to his left as the truck moved to their right.

The truck disappeared around the corner, and the shooting stopped.

"Are you okay, Meiling?"

"Yes. Thanks to you, sweetheart."

Ryan looked to his left and right, where four people lay against the concrete wall. "Is everyone okay?"

"I'm okay," Baker said. "How about you, Buck?"

"Let me think about that for a minute."

"I'm fine," Robert said. "But Ming has a cut on her arm from the glass."

"It's just a scratch, Robert. I'm fine too."

Ryan turned and entered the main door of the restaurant.

People were getting up from the floor.

Some kids were crying as mothers attempted to console them.

"Is anyone hurt in here?"

The manager said something in French, which sounded like he had repeated Ryan's message.

"*Nous allons bien.*" Came from someone on the floor.

Several people echoed the same message around the restaurant.

"We are all okay, except my window. This is not the first time this has happened, but the first time in a long time."

"We need to get out of here so we're not endangering these kids," Baker said.

"It was you, sir, they were trying to shoot?" the manager asked.

"No. It was me," Meiling said. "I am so sorry. We are leaving now, so you will all be safe."

"Who in Bambari wants us dead?" Ryan said.

"Whomever certain pharmaceutical companies paid to kill us," Meiling said.

Ryan had seen her temper before. She was near her boiling point. "Come on. We can talk about this on our way back to the hotel."

"I will talk about this right now. I am calling Colonel West to get President Warrington and the Secretary of State, James Wilson, on the line."

"The Secretary of State?" Robert's eyes widened. "Why?"

"I will ask him who the murderer is. Is it James Wilson or someone who works for him?"

"I am angry too, Meiling," Ryan tried to hook her arm.

She jerked it away. "But it is not ***you*** the people of Bambari think killed their friends and family."

"Our car is at the hotel," Baker said. "We need to get back there and then get out of Dodge before those dudes regroup to earn their money."

"We can talk as we walk back." Ryan nudged Meiling toward the street.

She didn't resist. That was a good sign.

After the six crossed the street and headed back to the hotel, the chatter started among them.

"Do you all remember our plan to flush out the guilty party or parties? It still works. It will identify whoever paid the would-be assassins."

"Maybe so," Meiling said. "But I will still call the president. They need to understand how serious this issue has become, and the Secretary of State needs to be pressured to find the traitors in his organization, and I am the one who will provide the pressure."

"Hey, bro," Baker said. "Remind me never to get on the wrong side of your wife."

"Can we stop discussing me?" Meiling's brow wrinkled again. "We need to discuss what we saw in the attack."

"We saw a fake UN pickup," Baker said. "And three guys with weapons the UN troops don't use."

"Rwanda and some of the other countries' troops deployed here use AK-47s, bro," Buck said. "But I agree, those were not peacekeepers who shot at us."

"Regardless, we need to kick it up a gear and get back to the hotel before those guys decide to try again." Baker strode out ahead of the group.

"What's back at the hotel to protect us?" Ryan tugged on Meiling's hand and tried to catch Baker.

"Our old beater with my M4 in the trunk. I can stand guard while the rest of you pack up so we can head for the airport."

Meiling, beside Ryan now, matched his fast pace. "But I need to stop by the hospital on the way out of town."

"Why? Did you leave something?" Ryan said.

"No. But I need to leave something. The killer protein for those still sick in quarantine at the hospital."

"It could save lives, and you forgot it?"

"Ryan, I didn't know we would be leaving this soon. I planned to leave it when Nurse Adamu realizes she can trust me. If I left it before that, she probably would have tossed the killer protein in the hazardous waste bin."

When the six strode into the hotel driveway, Baker headed toward the rented car. "Buck, my bag is packed. If you'll get it for me, I'll stand watch for those fake peacekeepers."

"Will do. Holler if those dudes show up again."

"You can count on it," Baker said as he opened the trunk.

Five minutes later, all six had squeezed into the old, beat-up Toyota sedan and, with Buck at the wheel, were headed down Route Nationale 2 (RN2) toward the hospital en route to the airport.

Meiling leaned forward and pointed out the driver-side window. "Park over there, Buck. I'll do this as quickly as possible, but this is a sensitive transaction. It might take a few minutes."

Meiling slid out of the back seat.

"Don't dillydally, Meiling," Baker said. "There's no place to hide the car. We're sitting ducks out here."

"They don't have any reason to associate you with this car, do they?" Meiling didn't wait for a reply. She turned and scurried toward the hospital office with her bag in hand.

Baker mumbled something to himself and shook his head. "Nope. There's no reason to associate us with this car, except it's the only rental in Bambari."

***

Meiling entered the office and waited for the administrator to look up from the papers on his desk.

"Dr. Chen-Adams, do you have more work to do in the lab?"

"No. My lab work is finished. But I have something that I need to give to Nurse Adamu. Will you get her for me, please?"

"Just a moment." He stood and left the room and returned in a couple of minutes with the nurse following him.

"I thought you were finished here." A scowl had formed on the nurse's face as she addressed Meiling.

"I almost was. Three gunmen targeted me while our team was at lunch. No one was injured. You might have heard the shooting at about half past twelve."

"I did. Why are you here?"

"How many Marburg patients do you have in quarantine now?"

"Thirteen."

Meiling pulled the box containing the vials of the killer protein from her bag. "This is enough to treat thirty patients."

"mAbs have to be cooled. If it has been in your duffle bag for the past twenty-four hours, it probably will do as much good as your shipment that killed two hundred and thirty-five of our people."

"We know now why the mAbs were ineffective. They were cooked en route by someone who wanted people to die here. We are investigating, and those responsible will be tried for murder."

The nurse opened her mouth to respond.

Meiling cut her off. "Please, listen to me. These are not mAbs vials. They contain my Marburg killer protein, and there are instructions for using them inside the box."

"How do they kill the virus, if that is even possible?"

"I have developed and tested a theory of manipulating the entire class of RNA viruses. I have been hesitant to publish my findings because they also provide quick methods of implementing gain of function. I fear they would be used to develop biowarfare weapons by CCP and terrorist groups."

The nurse's eyes said she was not buying what Meiling was telling her.

"Look. Try these infusions. What do you have to lose? If the patient is not into organ failure, the killer protein will reduce their viral load to zero over a twenty-four- or a forty-eight-hour period, depending on how sick they are."

"Have you saved lives using this killer protein?"

"Yes. We saved President Warrington's press secretary and three members of our team at our laboratory. This protein is now being distributed along with the mAbs to countries worldwide to treat those critically ill with the Novel Marburg Virus. To the best of my knowledge, no one has died of this virus if they were treated with the killer protein before their organs began to fail. After their viral load is reduced to near zero, you must follow the detox instructions that I included. That will remove the mRNA from the patients' bodies, so it doesn't continue to replicate."

Meiling set her bag down and laid a hand on the nurse's shoulder. "Please use this. Too many people have already died here. The dying must end now."

Meiling tried to read Nurse Adamu's eyes but noticed they were tear-filled. Then they overflowed.

She drew the nurse into a warm hug. "I almost lost my husband to another virus. This is the technique I used to save his life. It will save other lives here. My sat phone number is on the card in the box. Call me if you have any questions. You can reach me twenty-four-seven, as long as I'm not flying. May I have a number to contact you to see how the patients are doing?"

"Yes. You can call the administrator's number." She stepped back and met Meiling's gaze. "You know, when you pulled out the box, I intended to—"

"To throw it in the hazardous waste bin." Meiling giggled. "I thought that might be your reaction."

Nurse Adamu laughed too. "We will start the infusions as soon as we have read your instructions."

"Good. And we will contact the hospital as soon as we have charged those guilty of murdering all those people at your hospital. Then you can contact their families to inform them that the guilty are being brought to justice."

The nurse gave Meiling another hug.

"I have a question for you. I know that anti-government forces attacked the hospital. Do you think the hospital would have been attacked if you successfully treated the sick?"

"Some here in Bambari would think that was a good reason to attack us. They would rather see our people die."

"Do the peacekeepers provide the hospital with special security?"

"They are here, but only part of the time."

"You will get another mAbs shipment soon. I will order it today. But you must request full-time protection from the

UN troops. There are other people, people not in Bambari, who want the sick here to die."

"Who are those people?"

"I must not reveal that now. It could bring you more danger." Meiling paused. "Can you preserve for a few weeks the evidence we examined?"

"We can preserve the infusion evidence. But the people will want to bury their dead family members."

"Yes. You are right. We will use the photos and notes we made about the bodies we examined. I am so sorry this happened to your people, and I hope our discoveries here can prevent it from happening anywhere else ... I must go now. My team is waiting for me and watching in case the gunmen return."

When Meiling returned to the car, Buck had moved it to a shady spot along the road.

She saw five heads scanning the entire area around them through the open windows. It was a good sign.

Meiling slid into the seat behind the driver.

Baker twisted in his seat to face her. "What took you so long? We were beginning to think you had become another body in the morgue."

"I had to convince the head nurse that I was not a lying murderer before she would agree to administer the killer protein."

"Is that all?" Baker gave her a cheesy grin. "So she agreed?"

"She did. Now let's get—what do you call it—out of Dodge?"

Buck hit the accelerator, and they headed down RN2 toward the airport.

During the four-mile trip to the Bambari Airport, Meiling's pent-up anger seethed and boiled as she contemplated the traitorous, murderous acts by State Department employees.

After Buck parked the old Toyota near the Gulfstream, the five passengers slid out.

"I'll return the car to that spot beside the terminal like they asked. Be back in five minutes."

"Baker, may I use the Iridium phone in the cockpit while we wait for Buck?"

"Sure. What for?"

"I am calling Colonel West to report on what we found."

"I guess we should report in," Baker said.

Ryan studied her eyes for a moment. "Meiling, I don't like that look. What are you up to?"

She did not reply.

Baker unlocked the plane, deployed the steps, and they carried their bags inside.

Meiling headed for the cockpit.

"Wait until I power this bird up. Then you can use the phone."

When the power came on, Meiling took the phone and keyed in West's number.

Baker's voice came from behind her. "You do realize what time it is in D.C.?"

"I do not care what time it is in D.C."

"It's not quite 7:00 a.m." Baker slid into the pilot seat.

Colone West answered on the fourth ring.

"This is Meiling."

"How did the trip and the investigation go?"

"I can tell you that after you get President Warrington and Secretary of State James Wilson on the line."

"That's a tall order for 7:00 a.m. It would be a tall order any time of day.

"Do it, West. Someone in the State Department murdered two hundred and thirty-five innocent Africans in Bambari. Heads are going to bounce."

"I think you mean roll," Baker said.

"That's awful, Meiling," West said.

"It could get much worse. Right now, these murders could be happening all over the world. I must talk to the president and the Secretary of State now!"

Chapter 8

2:10 p.m., Bambari Airport

Meiling waited on hold while Colonel West tried to contact the president and the Secretary of State. Even if West reached them, there was no guarantee they would both be available.

Please, God, make them available. They need to hear this for the sake of the people in Bambari, the American people, and people of all nations where we are distributing our mAbs.

After two minutes, the line went live, and the colonel returned to the call. "Meiling, we're waiting for President Warrington to join the conference call I set up. It might be a few more minutes. James Wilson is already on the call. He's not happy, but he's on and waiting. I'll patch you in as soon as the president joins the call."

"So Secretary Wilson is not happy? He will be a lot less happy when I tell him what he is responsible for."

"Let me give you some advice, Meiling. Wilson has a bit of a temper. It's best to treat him with kid gloves."

"Kid gloves? That is not going to happen. I feel like putting horseshoes in my gloves and pounding some sense into him. If you could have seen what—"

"Hang on, Meiling. The president is joining the call."

Meiling's line went silent.

If James Wilson were angry because she disrupted his morning with the little matter of two hundred and thirty-five murders performed by people in his department, then she would give him a real reason to get mad.

The line went live again. “This is President Warrington. Are you there, Meiling?”

“I am here, Mr. President. Are you ready to hear the report from Bambari?”

“Please give us your report, Ms. Chen-Adams. I’ve got an important matter to tend to this morning.”

That must be James Wilson’s voice.

“Secretary Wilson, the matter I am bringing you is probably going to take most of your time for a lot more than just this morning.”

“I created a system to deliver your therapeutics all over the globe. The system is working flawlessly. What more do you want from my department?” Wilson’s voice turned caustic on the last sentence.

“I want two of your pilots arrested for murder and a thorough investigation of your ***flawless system*** to identify and bring to justice all the accessories to murder.”

“Of all the—”

“Meiling, tell me what you found that would warrant such action.” President Warrington’s voice of authority took over the call that was rapidly running off the rails.

“Wendell, here’s what we found when—”

“Wendell? That’s not how we address the President of the United States. And why should I arrest my pilots who are flying the maximum hours allowed while trying to deliver your mongoloid antibodies?”

“It’s monoclonal antibodies, usually referred to as mAbs. Mr. President, here is what we found in Bambari—indisputable evidence that the mAbs were cooked by one or both pilots en route to Bambari. That completely destroyed their efficacy with the result that the two hundred and thirty-five people from Bambari who were given the infusions died from the Novel Marburg Virus. We examined the mAbs used and the corpses of the dead in the morgue at the regional hospital in Bambari.”

"You are not going to blame my department and my pilots without a lot more evidence than just ***your*** opinion."

"It is the expert opinion of four world-class virologists. And if you examine the flight time and the log of the flight from Minneapolis to Bambari on May twentieth, I am sure you will find an additional stop somewhere in the Continental U.S. and a refueling stop in Casablanca that took much longer than necessary to simply refuel the Gulfstream. I will stake my job and my career on it. How about you, Mr. Secretary."

"That's enough, Meiling," President Warrington said. "These are serious charges that have international implications for the handling of this pandemic. Many, many lives are at stake. James, I want you to start this investigation immediately and personally stay on top of it. You will brief me on your progress and findings each evening."

"Mr. President, is this alleged incident that serious?"

"Secretary Wilson," Meiling cut in. "It was serious to the people of Bambari. Do you want me to describe to you in detail what happens when you die of Marburg? These people weren't just murdered; they were tortured to death. Is this what the U.S. State Department has come to stand for?"

"Please spare us the description, Ms. Chen-Adams."

"It's ***Dr.*** Chen-Adams, Secretary Wilson. And if you try to downplay this incident, we will all, as my husband says, find ourselves on our way to Hades in a handbasket."

"Meiling, no one will downplay these murders," the president said. "Not on my watch. Did you have any other significant findings from your Bambari trip?"

"Yes. When we arrived at the regional hospital, the staff despised me. They blamed me for the deaths. If word gets out, the media will blame me, and they will blame the administration, including the State Department.

"It took a lot of persuasion for hospital staff to cooperate with us. But worse than that, this same method of murder could happen again anywhere the conspirators want it to happen. We must make sure it cannot happen. I propose having an appropriate trusted authority, perhaps a U.S. Marshall, onboard each flight to ensure the integrity of the mAbs.

"Regarding the Bambari flight, we need to know where the plane stopped and for how long. Who were the pilots? Who was their supervisor? We must know each State Department member involved in the Bambari shipment. What connections did they have to the big pharmaceutical companies."

"Hold it, Dr. Chen-Adams. Why are you—"

"Mr. Secretary, someone sent fake U.N peacekeepers to kill me. Three men armed with automatic weapons emptied their magazines less than thirty meters from our entire Bambari team. Only the quick reactions of my husband and our pilot saved the six of us. And this was not the locals seeking revenge. Those responsible appear to be people who would benefit from my being removed from the pandemic effort. And I am sure they did not want me to return to D.C. and give the president this report."

Secretary Wilson did not reply.

"James, you ***will*** conduct this investigation, and it ***will*** provide answers to Meiling's questions," the president said. "All guilty parties, regardless of their organizational affiliations, even if they are state actors, must be brought to justice. If not, Mr. Secretary, you will be looking for another job. Have I made myself clear?"

"Yes, Mr. President."

Chapter 9

11:15 p.m. EDT, Phisher Pharmaceuticals Headquarters, East Manhattan

Abe Borland, CEO of Phisher Pharmaceuticals pulled his secure private phone from his desk and called the secure phone of the CDC Chief Operating Officer Dr. Marshall McDowell. McDowell needed to know what had happened and hear an explanation of the bad news.

"This is Marsh McDowell."

"Marsh, this is Abe. The State Department has an investigation going on the department's delivery of mAbs to Bambari."

"I'm part of the federal government, Abe. Not you. So how do you know this when I do not?"

"We have our sources in the State Department. Let's leave it at that. But we haven't accomplished our goal yet. And we cannot risk another mAbs cooking lesson. They're onto that. In addition, we will soon lose our two pilot chefs because of the investigation."

Marsh swore. "Is there any way the investigators can trace this back to us?"

"Of course not. We're too far removed."

"They could say we have a motive."

Abe chuckled. "If anyone tries to push that in the media, it will fly right back in their face. It's not a politically correct message."

"Who figured this out, and how did they do it so quickly?"

"Little Ms. Chen-Adams, the lady who's too smart for her own good. She also survived the ***'terrorist'*** attack in Bambari."

Marsh cursed again, slighting the character of the Chinese virologist. "Trying to put Dr. Chen-Adams in disfavor didn't work, and she survived an assassination attempt. So how do we purge the little pest?"

"This calls for extreme measures. We must move on to plan B."

"Remind me what plan B entails and why it was plan B rather than plan A."

Abe sighed into the phone. "It was plan B because it was an extreme measure. The plan's premise was that if Pierce's lab and all the people in it were destroyed in a terrorist attack, with our vaccine that is entering testing now, we would find ourselves in the driver's seat for treating the Marburg Pandemic. President Warrington would have no good choice but to turn to us."

"I don't know," Marsh said. "Warrington could continue allowing MABS International and ProtSyn to manufacture the mAbs and Chen-Adams's killer protein. They could tap a competent virologist to update the hybridoma when the virus mutated too far and continue manufacturing with the new hybridoma."

"We could also hit the two manufacturing plants with the terror attack. But, Marsh, with the influence of that Chinese honeypot gone and forgotten, we could step in and replace her and make all policy decisions going forward. As to what plan B entails, it requires a meeting with General Kuo, the North American Commander of the PLA. We must also coordinate the effort with the Deputy Director of the FBI."

"I know plan B is a terrorist attack, but who did we decide should get the blame for that atrocity?"

"The CCP and their PLA cohorts will conduct the apparent terrorist attack with the help of hand-picked FBI agents. We will blame the radical environmental and population-control group Global Threat Initiative (GTI). Phisher and the CDC will express their outrage at a terrorist attack from a radical group that wants to depopulate the planet."

"Then, shouldn't we call General Kuo right now?"

"Yes. And we need to call the FBI Deputy Director, Harold Stein. Let me see if I can reach them."

Abe had both Stein and General Kuo on a conference call within five minutes.

"This had better be important, Abe. We've had nothing but manure hitting the fan since Meiling Chen-Adams returned from the Central African Republic."

"Scraping her off the walls is what this call is about, Harold. We are moving ahead with plan B. How many men can you contribute?"

"I have twenty men we can count on, agents who support what we're doing."

"General Kuo, it is good to have you with us," Abe said. "If we launch plan B ASAP, how many men can you contribute?"

"I also have about twenty men. They are trustworthy PLA men from our Chinese police stations in American cities—Los Angeles, San Francisco, and New York. The New York station was, unfortunately, closed by the Warrington administration, but that gives us all of New York's men."

"And, General Kuo, you were supplying the arms for us. Do we have everything we will need?"

"Yes. North Korea and Iran were most helpful in that regard."

"Okay, gentlemen, we are initiating plan B. Tell your people to be on alert. We will move out as soon as we see that all the targets are at Pierce's lab. I will call you both when that happens."

"Harold, please stay on the line for a few minutes. I have another matter I need to talk to you about."

"Sure, Abe. I've got a few minutes before my next meeting."

"Good." Abe waited a few seconds until the other men had dropped off the conference call. "I didn't want to have this discussion with General Kuo on the line."

"What's this all about, Abe?"

"We need a plan C."

"Seriously?"

"Yes, seriously."

"Okay. Why do we need plan C, what does it entail, and why do you want to cut General Kuo out of this plan?"

"We need a plan C only for the remote possibility that plan B might fail."

"Suppose plan B did fail," Harold said. "Kuo's men are Asian, and my men are American but a mix of races. They carry no ID, and all have GTI uniforms. If any are killed or captured, the authorities will think they are GTI members or mercenaries hired by GTI."

"I agree," Abe said. "But if the lab continues to operate, the only way we can shut down Meiling Chen-Adams's operation is to take out the factories she's using."

"I see why you wouldn't want Kuo involved. If some Asian terrorists killed several former Wuhan lab scientists, that's not as big a deal as some Chinese attacking an American manufacturing plant working on a government project. If anyone figured out they were PLA, that could start a war."

"I'm glad we agree, Harold. Now, do you have some men who could damage the two plants so they could not operate for months?"

"I do, but they would need some time to study the facilities to determine the best ways to incapacitate them."

"At a minimum, what is enough time?"

"I would say about two weeks."

"What if they only had two or three days?"

"Then they would need much more powerful explosives. It would be harder to obtain them and much trickier to deploy them. There would likely be collateral damage—buildings outside the plant and possible chemical or biological contamination. There would be more danger to the men during the assault, the explosions, and the escape—especially during the escape."

The next question would reveal the depth of Harold's resolve to accomplish the goals they had envisioned for the Marburg Pandemic. "What if we didn't want them to escape?"

"Are you suggesting a suicide mission?"

"Just consider the men collateral damage, necessary collateral damage."

"Abe, these men aren't stupid. They would spot any excessive danger to them in the plan. They would refuse to participate. They would never trust me again, and they might try to assassinate me."

"I was simply brainstorming, and that was a bad idea. Forget I suggested it."

"If we could get some building plans or factory drawings, we could devise a plan to get some men in, cripple the factory with fewer explosives, and get out. A team of ten men could accomplish that."

"But we need two factories taken out."

"Then we need two teams."

"And the assaults will have to be simultaneous."

"You're making this difficult, Abe."

"Nothing worthwhile is easy."

Harold's pensive expression said Abe was winning the war of wills.

Now for the clencher. "I will get you some building plans. You'll have them by sometime tomorrow."

"And how will you do that?"

"I have friends in Minnesota, government people."

"Don't give me the details. The less I know about it, the better." Harold paused. "We will need a ploy to gather a group of men near the factories without drawing suspicion. Perhaps they could be road or utility maintenance people ... until it gets dark."

"Can you station the men at both the MABS International site in Minneapolis and the ProtSyn site in Rochester in less than forty-eight hours?"

"I'll have to call in my special forces."

"Do you mean the HRT?"

"No. Word would leak out if I tried to use the Hostage Rescue Team. I will call my people trained for black operations. They are used to working undercover and are tight-lipped if there are any investigations."

"Sounds good. To whom do I send the building plans?"

"I will give you contact information for the two team leaders after I've selected the teams. We have a secure drop box where you can leave the files. The drop box login info will be with the contact information."

"Since I've got some action items with a short fuse, I must go now. We will talk again if problems arise. If not, I will talk to you shortly before the assault."

They ended the call.

Chapter 10

The next day, 07:55 a.m., Rocky Mountain Metro, Colorado

Meiling took a seat next to Ryan in Dr. Pierce's van. She laid her head on Ryan's shoulder and then focused on Baker in the passenger seat in front of her. "Baker, thanks for giving us a good night's sleep at the Sky Airport Hotel in Casablanca. I was exhausted after the events of the day." Meiling yawned. "After fourteen hours on the plane, I'm ready for another nap."

"No problem, Meiling," Baker said. "There were going to be delays in getting fuel, and I thought we could all use a shower and a nap after examining bodies in a morgue, rolling in the dirt to keep from being shot, and spending a hot summer day in Bambari."

Buck shoved the van into gear, rolled across the tarmac, and headed toward the highway.

"We'll be home in fifteen minutes, sweetheart," Ryan said. "You can have a nap then if you need one. But you know something?"

"What?"

"You didn't complain about morning sickness the whole time we've been traveling."

Meiling smiled. "There was too much going on, too much adrenaline flowing. I didn't have time to think about being sick. But you know something?"

"What, sweetheart?"

"You should not have mentioned it. I am starting to feel queasy again." She straightened in her seat. "Buck, please don't dillydally on our way home, or you might regret it."

"Not to worry, Meiling. We'll be pushing the speed limit all the way."

The van made the left turn and surged forward onto Highway 128.

"Meiling, have you forgotten the issues we left behind when we ran off to Bambari?"

She laid her head on his shoulder again. "I do not want to think about them, Ryan. Certainly not now. I need to be still."

Ten minutes later, Buck turned the van onto the long driveway leading to the lab.

"Buck, do you recognize that car sitting at our gate," Baker said.

"No. At least it's not blocking the gate. But isn't that one of those Colorado fleet license plates?"

Meiling raised her head a few inches. "Please tell me it is not someone from the state coming to harass me."

"Can't tell yet, Meiling. The dude just got out, and he has a big envelope in one hand."

"Make him go away." Meiling moaned the words.

Ryan's body tensed. "If you don't, Baker, I will."

Baker glanced back at Ryan. "Whatever you're thinking, bro, those eyes say you're headed for trouble. Maybe for a jail cell. Let me handle this. I believe I can make this dude go away."

She circled Ryan with her arms and held him with a firm grip. "Let Baker handle it, Ryan. I don't want you to get in trouble too."

"Buck," Ryan said. "Stop the van in front of the gate, but don't open it yet."

"You got it."

After the van stopped, the stranger sauntered up to the driver-side window.

Buck waved him around to the passenger side window.

Baker had the window down. "What's up, dude?"

“I have something to deliver to Meiling Chen-Adams. I thought she would get in yesterday evening, but she didn’t show, so I had to drive back down here this morning.”

“Who told you we would get back yesterday evening?”

“That’s none of your business.”

“Look, dude. We got ambushed by a team of assassins with automatic weapons yesterday. So any stranger hanging around ***is*** our business.” Baker turned toward Dr. Pierce and Ming, sitting in the rear seat. “Grab my M4 for me, Robert.”

Pierce handed the gun to Ryan, who gave it to Baker.

Baker loaded a bullet in the chamber, causing a loud metallic click.

“Hold on a minute. I’m an attorney working for the Colorado State Attorney General’s office, here on official business.”

Baker pointed the barrel of the gun slightly to the man’s right. “And you’re looking at the official business end of my M4. Now tell us what you’re really here for.”

“I have a subpoena that I must deliver personally to Ms. Meiling Chen-Adams.”

“Do you mean to ***Dr***. Meiling Chen-Adams, Director of the United States Marburg Pandemic Response Team, who reports directly to President Warrington?”

“Titles are irrelevant. I need to know if she’s on this van.”

“Dude, do you know where every person on this van just came from?”

“I heard that you went to the Central African Republic. But that’s irrelevant.”

“Irrelevant? Do you know what we did there?”

“No. And I don’t care. Just—”

“Don’t care? Perhaps I can inject some caring into that thick head of yours.”

The man jerked his head back as if he had been slapped.

"Don't play offended with me. I'm in no mood for it," Baker said. "Two hundred and thirty-five people died of Marburg. We went there to do autopsies, determine what killed them, and do some more tasks you ***don't care*** about. That virus kills ninety percent of the people it infects. By the way, have you been infused with Dr. Chen-Adams's monoclonal antibodies."

The man backed a few steps away from the van. "No. They are not giving it prophylactically yet."

"That's too bad. You see, we were knee-deep in Novel Marburg deaths yesterday and haven't decontaminated in our lab yet. This little bug is airborne. They say it can travel thirty to sixty feet and hang in the air for ten to twenty minutes."

The man backed farther away from the van.

"We're all immune to Marburg, except for Buck, our driver. He hasn't been treated yet."

Buck began a prolonged coughing spasm that sounded like someone at the near-death end of emphysema.

Meiling tried not to giggle or laugh, but she couldn't hold it in. After her first guffaw, she couldn't hold anything in.

She jumped up from her seat, opened the van door, and splattered her last meal in the general direction of the attorney.

"Projectile vomiting! She's got it again!" Baker yelled. "Robert, she needs another infusion."

A terrified squeal erupted from the intruder's mouth as he turned and ran for his vehicle.

Screaming tires spun on the driveway pavement when the state vehicle backed up. Then it roared down the driveway toward the street.

"Great job, Buck," Baker said.

"Yeah, way to go, Buck," Ryan said.

Meiling climbed into the van and sat beside Ryan.

"Great timing, Meiling. And I'm taking bets. Odds are five to one that he mails that subpoena this time."

"Let's go check on Lee and Jinghua," Meiling said. "Then it's time for breakfast. I am hungry."

Chapter 11

08:30 a.m., Pierce's lab compound

After Buck parked the van inside the compound, Ryan opened the door and held Meiling's hand as she climbed out.

As soon as she stepped onto the asphalt of the parking area, her hand went to her stomach.

"Are you getting nauseous again?"

"Maybe a little. Or maybe I just need to eat something."

Ryan glanced toward the lab when the lobby door opened.

Jinghua and Lee headed their way.

Ming and Robert climbed out of the van behind Ryan and Meiling.

Baker and Buck joined them, and the entire team of eight stood by the van.

"Robert, something happened here yesterday." The tone Lee used made his statement sound ominous.

"Yes," Jinghua said. "We believe we have a security issue to address."

"What happened?" Ryan said.

Lee pointed to a spot where the trees came within fifty yards of the lab. "Those trees provide a clear view of the lab door, less than fifty meters from it. A man carrying a shotgun walked out from the trees and raised his gun to shoot …"

"Well, did he shoot?" Robert asked.

"No," Jinghua said. "He lowered his gun without shooting it."

"I talked to the man," Lee said. "He claimed he was a pheasant hunter. And it appeared he was. A dog ran out from the trees and joined him."

His story sounded rather fishy. "This is June," Ryan said. "It's not open season for any game birds."

"But some of the farmers hunt out of season around here," Robert said.

"But if a farmer with a gun can get that close to our lab undetected, they could shoot any of us as we walk across the parking area to the lab," Lee said.

"I see his point." Baker blew out a long sigh. "Buck and I can take care of part of that problem tomorrow. We'll get an infrared security system with video and surround the lab with well-placed, hidden sensors. We just need to decide where to put the cameras."

"You said ***part*** of the problem," Ryan said. "Are you thinking we need to hire a security guard to monitor the system?"

"That's exactly what I'm thinking, especially after the attack on us yesterday in Bambari."

Jinghua sighed. "I guess any time you become known worldwide, there are people who do not like you."

"You are wise, Xiǎo nǚ'ér," Lee said.

Jinghua gave Lee a warm smile.

Meiling nudged Ryan and leaned close. "Did you hear that, sweetheart?"

"Yes, but I'm not sure what Lee said."

She tiptoed to whisper to him. "He called Jinghua his ***little daughter***. That is a good sign."

And it was a good sign. In less than three months in a free country with free access to a Bible, which he now read often, Dr. Li had become the man God meant him to be. He was no longer the hardened Communist scientist but had become a friend and a trusted member of their team. And though Lee hadn't officially told Ryan yet, all indications were that Lee was now a devoted Jesus follower.

Baker gave Lee and Jinghua a cheesy grin. "Moving along with the security issue Lee raised—Rafer can have the Huey here in ten minutes from the time we notify him. That's okay if we have a large group coming to attack us. But what if we have a sniper in the woods trying to pick us off?"

"We need the system monitored twenty-four-seven," Robert said.

"Yes, and Rafer might know where we can get a couple of reliable security guards. He knows some retired vets in this area. If it's okay with everyone, I'll check with him tomorrow."

"And I'll call Colonel West today to request budget to pay them," Robert said.

"A word of caution," Ryan said. "If West suggests using federal guards—FBI or Secret Service—tell him we have too many enemies hiding in the federal government. We'd feel more comfortable and would be safer with guards we choose."

Robert motioned toward the trees. "How do we respond to a sniper in the woods?"

"Buck and I both have special forces training. We can do a little sniping ourselves. I've got my M4, and I know where we can pick up a legal M1A sniper's rifle. But there will be times when Buck and I are away in the Gulfstream."

"Can we ensure the guards we hire are proficient with a sniper's rifle?" Ryan said.

"Since we're looking for guards among vets, we can probably do that. But it would be good to give all the men here some training on using an M1A."

Ming poked Baker's shoulder. "Baker, I do not want to miss the fun."

"Okay," Baker said. "Ming will be sniper-trained too."

***

11:30 a.m. ET, Phisher Pharmaceuticals Headquarters, East Manhattan

Abe Borland's secure phone rang. He glanced at the display. This could be the call he'd been waiting for.

"Borland here."

"Abe, this is Winningham. I only saw the old Asian guy when I was there yesterday. But today, all eight of the staff are at the lab. I'll let you know if anyone leaves."

"I want all of them to be there two days from now. So watch who comes and who goes, and try to keep track of who is on-site, especially Meiling Chen-Adams. If she and Pierce are both at the lab in two days, I'll give the green light for plan B."

Chapter 12

10:30 a.m. the next day, Pierce's lab, Conference room

Meiling pushed a red stickpin into New Zealand on the world map mounted on the wall of the conference room. "I expect New Zealand to have problems now that they have reported confirmed cases of Novel Marburg. They did not fare well during the COVID Pandemic due to excessive and unreasonable government interference with what should have been medical professionals' decisions. Regardless, they have received their first shipment of mAbs."

Robert shuffled a stack of papers on the table in front of him. "I have the most recent weekly reports from fifteen countries. Where shall we begin?"

"Did Bambari report?" Ming asked.

"Yes," Robert said. "It's short, but they did file a report."

Meiling took her seat. "Good. Let's start with Bambari."

"They infused twelve patients at the hospital with the killer protein Meiling gave them, and the patients' viral loads are dropping rapidly. The mAbs shipment should arrive tomorrow morning."

"Thank goodness things are under control now at the regional hospital," Meiling said.

"Thank goodness you had the men with you over there," Jinghua said and sighed.

Ming gave her a twisted smile. "Especially men like Buck McKinney? Or were you wishing Buck had remained here at the lab?"

Jinghua gave Ming a mock frown. "Why are you asking me about Buck?"

Meiling laughed. "Because you were making—how do we say it in America—***gaga eyes*** at him this morning."

"I was not." Jinghua directed her frown at Meiling. "By the way, who is Buck McKinney, and why is he here? I know he is a pilot, but ..."

"Yes, he is a pilot. But since he is Baker's friend from Oregon, Jinghua, you should visit Baker's wife, Shauna, and ask her. They all live in Redmond, or they did until the Marburg outbreak."

Jinghua nodded.

"Robert cleared his throat. "If we've heard the skinny on Buck McKinney, perhaps we can finish discussing Bambari."

Meiling turned her attention back to Robert. "I think we are finished with Bambari. What is next?"

Robert lifted another paper from the stack on the table. "Here's the report from India comparing the effectiveness of recent mAbs treatments to the earlier mAbs derived from the plasmablasts. It says that while the plasmablasts saved lives, the B-cells produced later in the infection seem to stop it more efficiently."

"Speaking of the men," Jinghua said. "Where are they this morning?"

Ming gave Jinghua another smirk. "Who is speaking of the men?"

"Look," Robert said. "One of the men is sitting with you at this table with a report from India in his hands. Dr. Li is working in the BSL-4 lab this morning, and the other three are trying to install a wireless-camera-based security system around the perimeter of our property."

"I see." Jinghua leaned her head on one hand, trying to shield her reddened face from Robert's view.

***

11:00 a.m., Ryan's weather station in Pierce's lab

Ryan sat at his small desk in his weather station, analyzing the Boulder sounding and a lifted index chart to see if there might be thunderstorms in the area this afternoon. Baker and Buck planned to deploy the sensors and cameras for the lab's new wireless security camera system, and thunderstorm activity could interfere with setting up the security network.

The lifted index was minus one, indicating only a slight chance of thunderstorms.

The door to the weather lab swung open, revealing Baker with an armload of boxes.

Buck stood behind him also with a full load of boxes.

Ryan pointed to the only table in his lab. "I've only got a small table in here but pile your boxes on it."

Ryan steadied Baker's load as he set it on the table, then helped Buck place his load beside Baker's.

"Which box has the instruction manual?" Ryan waved his hand over the two piles of boxes.

"This one." Baker slid the top box from his stack, opened it, and pulled out a booklet the size of a small paperback novel.

Ryan took the manual and opened it to the table of contents. "The quick start guide is only five pages. Let's start there."

"Adams, got a question for you," Buck said.

Ryan looked up from the manual. "Shoot before I get engrossed in the system setup instructions."

"Uh, what's Jinghua's story? I heard she was in a bad situation when you rescued her from the Wuhan lab."

"She was sick with the Novel Marburg and locked in an isolation room when Ming found her. Formally, she's Dr. Jinghua Ren, a virologist with a couple of years of experience at the Wuhan lab. Not too shabby for a thirty-year-old."

"She's thirty?" Buck's voice rose half an octave on the last word. Then he blew out a long sigh.

"Yeah. Thirty. Though she looks like she's about eighteen." Ryan looked up and saw a smile forming on Buck's face. "That's her story. Why are you asking?"

"I noticed that Ming and Robert seemed to be joined at the hip. They're always together."

Baker chuckled. "Joined at the hip? I'm betting they'll be joined in holy matrimony before the summer's over. Robert has been a widower for three lonely years, and Ming thought she would never have a chance at marriage from a Christian man in China. She'd given up."

Buck turned toward Baker. "Where does Jinghua stand on that issue?"

Baker plopped a hand on Buck's shoulder. "You'll have to ask her that ... if you're man enough to do it."

"Bro, don't joke about things like that. This could be serious once-in-a-lifetime stuff."

Baker chuckled again. "Once in a lifetime? Dude, you're moving too fast. You might scare away a cute little thing like Jinghua."

"If you could use a little intelligence info, you might ask Meiling," Ryan said. "Don't ask Ming. She's as nutty as Baker. Tries to have fun all the time ... mostly at other people's expense." Ryan paused. "There's another person you will need to satisfy before you get any quality time with Jinghua."

"Another person here at the lab? Who? We've talked about nearly everybody."

Ryan shook his head. "Not everybody. And from what I heard yesterday, Lee has assumed the father role for Jinghua. He called her his ***little daughter***, in Chinese."

"In Chinese? How do you know that's what he said?"

"Meiling pointed it out to me. So you have a protective father to deal with. You'd better find out if Lee knows Kung Fu."

"Seriously? The guy is over sixty years old."

"Buck, you never know about those Asian men. Didn't you ever watch Karate Kid?" Ryan punched Buck's shoulder. "Come on. We've got a security system to set up."

"Right," Baker said. "We need our video to cover all of the potential sniper positions and all concealed approaches. There are the groves of trees, the rocky bluffs along Coal Creek, and the tall grass and bushes in the wildlife refuge to the south."

Ryan turned the page in the user's manual. "Before you two go galivanting around the countryside, let me connect the controller to the video screen. Then it looks like all I have to do is activate the receiver-transmitter. When you position a camera-sensor, just turn it on and it should sync with the system and give me a picture. The system determines where the cameras are by using their GPS coordinates and then uses those to superimpose them over a satellite picture of this area."

"What's the accuracy of the camera locations?" Baker asked.

"This is a high-quality system," Ryan said. "It locates positions of the sensors to within three meters. And I'll have a video display for each camera and a screen with the map and the camera positions numbered on the map. If someone is detected, I'll know where they are."

"When the system is up, and the cameras are in their final positions, we should generate a picture of the map and give it to Rafe so that we can direct him to the target locations," Baker said.

Buck laughed. "If Rafer is going to start blasting targets near our cameras, we need to buy a bunch of extras. If a large force ever attacked us, he'd probably blow up all our cameras."

"Based on what we saw the Huey Cobra do with its RPGs at the Utah Test and Training Range, I'd say your right," Baker said.

An hour later, Ryan sat watching cameras go live on the system as Baker and Buck distributed them in the trees and among the rocks surrounding the lab compound.

As the last camera came online, Ryan pulled out his cell and called Baker.

"Baker here. What's up, Ryan?"

"All the cameras are up. Where are you two?"

"I'm watching Buck try not to break his neck as he climbs down from the rock wall along Coal Creek."

"When he gets down, will you two walk up to the head of the driveway and then try to sneak back through the trees or along the creek without being caught by the system?"

"Sure. But we know where all the cameras are."

"Exactly. If you can't get through, the bad guys, who don't know where the cameras are, can't get through undetected either."

A loud buzz came through the phone. "What's going on out there, Baker?"

"Buck aggravated a rattlesnake on the rock. He bailed off the rock about ten feet up. The snake's quieting down now. Buck's not limping or anything. I guess all's well that ends well."

"Dude!" Buck's agitated voice came through the phone. "You should have warned me about the rattlesnakes."

"Bro, you're from Eastern Oregon. I figured you'd know. Except for your hair standing on end, it's all good.

"Right," Buck growled the word.

"Let's jog up to the head of the driveway and make like the bad guys trying to attack the lab. Ryan wants to test the system."

Fifteen minutes later, an alarm lit up when Buck appeared on camera nine. He had made it almost half of the way through the grove of trees to the east of the lab.

After another five minutes had elapsed, camera two had picked up Baker. He had reached a cluster of trees only three hundred yards from the compound.

Baker's Special Forces training and knowledge of the camera positions had almost put him in a position to snipe anyone walking through the compound. But an actual intruder, with no knowledge of the camera locations and the sensor network, would never make it as far as Baker had.

Ryan crammed a handful of potato chips into his mouth, crunched on them for a while, and swallowed. Then, he called Baker again. "You and Buck need to come in now. The system did its job, but now we need to see Rafer to tell him about the security system and get some names for potential security monitors."

"No, bro. Buck and I need to come in for lunch. It's after one o'clock, and we're starving."

Ryan crunched noisily on another handful of chips.

"Dude, you went to the vending machine and then sat with your rear end in your comfy office chair while we were out here dodging rattlesnakes."

"Supervisory privileges."

"And where did you get those?"

Ryan chuckled and crunched on another mouthful of chips. "From my wife. We all know Meiling runs this place."

"It's Pierce's lab, but Meiling does seem to call the shots," Baker said. "Speaking of calling, I'll call in a take-out order to the HangryHorse Café in Superior. We can pick it up on our way to Rafe's house."

Two hours later, Ryan, Baker, and Buck sat around the dining room table at Rafer Jackson's house.

Ryan had briefed Rafe on the new security system.

"The question is, can we get the Huey in position soon enough to stop an attack when it is detected," Ryan said.

Rafe sighed. "Yeah. After the president intervened, we did get permission to park our bird in a hangar that's quickly accessible if I'm driving in from my home."

He paused. "It takes five minutes to get here and five minutes to roll the pad out of the hangar and take off. I can fly five and a half miles to the lab in three minutes. If I'm at home, the best case is thirteen minutes from notification until I'm ready to engage the target."

Buck shook his head. "We really need another helicopter pilot, so we always have someone on standby."

Baker was now shaking his head. "What we need is for the military to take over the security for the lab."

"We can't rely on the military," Ryan said.

Buck's frowning face displayed unbelief. "Why is our military unreliable?"

"Are you aware of the leadership at the Pentagon, people mostly placed there by the previous administration?"

"I know they're not the best we've got, but still—"

"Buck, it's not their capability that's the problem. Just like Congress, a third have sold their souls to the CCP. Consequently, they have refused the president's request using phony excuses and burying it in bureaucratic red tape."

"If that's what we're up against, we're doomed."

"Damaged but not doomed. Until the president can kick the Commies and other Marxists out of positions of authority, patriotic people like Meiling, who's only been an American citizen for four months, and people like us must stand in the gap."

Baker laid a hand on Buck's shoulder. "It's not right, Buck. But that's how it's got to be until God and country are once again the highest priorities to Americans and the federal government."

"That's right, Buck," Ryan said. "We're civilians taking on a task that rightly belongs to our Defense Department. And at this juncture, the DOD is acting more like our enemy. We're on our own to protect the lab."

"Moving right along," Baker said. "Rafe, did you get a chance to contact any vets around here who would be willing to monitor our security system for the lab?"

"Yeah. I got more interested vets than I could handle. Here are the top four." Rafer handed Baker a sheet with notes about each applicant and their contact information.

Baker reached for his cell. "Mind if I call them from here, Rafe?"

"Go right ahead. Sounds like you need some help immediately."

When they left Rafer Jackson's house at 4:00 p.m., Ryan had two great candidates for security monitors, Jack Jordan and Bill Reynolds. They would even be helpful if, heaven forbid, the fighting reached the compound.

At 5:15 a.m., the two men would report to Ryan for OJT on the security system. Shortly after that, the lab would be ready for anything except an attack from the air. And that was highly unlikely.

Chapter 13

7:00 p.m. EDT, Abe Borland's Office, Phisher Pharmaceuticals Headquarters

Abe's secure phone rang its annoying ringtone. Maybe his annoyances were about to be erased. "Borland here."

"Abe, this is Winningham. The three men who've been gone all afternoon just returned. All eight of the staff are at the lab now. It's dinnertime, so I expect them to remain at the lab for the rest of the night."

"Good work, Winningham."

"There's something else you ought to know."

"What's that."

Winningham cleared his throat. "Well, uh, two of those three men spent a few hours today roaming around the trees and the creek near the lab. I couldn't see exactly where they were or what they did, but ..."

"Yes, but ..." Abe stroked his chin briefly. "Do you suppose they were increasing security around the lab?"

"Could be, but I don't see how that helps them if a superior force overruns them," Winningham said.

"You're probably right, as long as they weren't mining the area or planting other nasty traps."

"As I said, I couldn't see them often, but it didn't look like they were carrying mines or other explosives."

"Thanks, Winningham. I'll tell the men to move in cautiously. We certainly don't want them blown up by booby traps and alerting everyone at the lab compound. Winningham, I want you to stay in sight of the head of the lab's driveway tonight and let me know if anyone leaves. You can leave when our troops arrive."

"Yes, sir. Mind if I stay and watch the war in the morning?"

"No. As long as you stay out of the way. Report to me when the first troops arrive, then you can do as you wish."

Abe ended the call and initiated another call, a video conference with Marshall McDowell, CDC Chief Operating Officer, General Kuo, PLA North American Commander, and FBI Deputy Director Harold Stein.

"Gentlemen, all the subjects are present and accounted for. We execute plan B with the attack starting at daybreak, 5:30 a.m. local time in Colorado. Are you all prepared?"

"My troops are ready and anxious to accomplish something meaningful in the U.S.," General Kuo said.

"Likewise for my select team of FBI," Harold Stein said.

"But there is one new development for which I must inform you." Abe waited for a response.

They didn't reply.

"Two men from the lab were seen today moving through the trees around the compound. We don't know what they were up to, but I suggest we move in cautiously in case they were booby trapping the area."

"Duly noted," Stein said.

"Regarding the purpose of this mission," Abe said, "we want everyone inside the compound killed. And the lab destroyed."

General Kuo shook his head.

Marsh McDowell gave Abe a bug-eyed stare. "You're crazy, Abe. No one on this team of forty men will blow up a level four lab. Who knows what the men would be contaminating themselves with? We will take out the infrastructure that supports the lab and destroy some of the buildings, but not the biosafety areas themselves."

Abe knew he had committed a gross oversight, so he didn't reply. Had he really devalued the men putting boots on the ground so much that he thought nothing of exposing them to deadly pathogens? He wanted to tell himself no. But he knew the truth. He did not value these men's lives beyond completing this mission.

Abe was once an MD. He had taken an oath and then forgotten it as the drive for profits overshadowed all other concerns. He was guilty, but Abe would not admit it to these men.

What did it matter that the biosafety areas remained? They would have no infrastructure to support them, and the people who ran them would die. That should be sufficient to force President Warrington to rely on Phisher Pharmaceuticals.

"Abe?" Marsh was staring at him. "Did you hear?"

"That's fine, Marsh. No, we can't touch the biosafety areas. With most of the lab damaged and the people dead, this lab will be decontaminated and destroyed. Given that it was once a functioning BSL-4 lab, no one will want to use this property for the next several years."

Marsh nodded but still looked concerned.

Abe sighed. "Let's all go home and get a good night's sleep so we can turn Pierce's lab compound into a ghost town in the morning."

Chapter 14

5:30 a.m., Ryan's weather station inside the lab building

Ryan had walked Jack and Bill, the two security monitors, through the system's operation. Now it was their turn to demonstrate their ability to use the system.

Ryan stepped away from the control computer and motioned Jack to move in. "Jack, start monitoring the system from the farthest cameras to the east of the lab and working your way to the nearest cameras. Enlarge the video from each camera, one at a time, as you work your way in. You can stop and study the screen if you see anything interesting."

"Got it." Jack enlarged the video from camera twenty, displaying it on the big control panel monitor. "Uh, Ryan? Are you springing something unexpected on us to see how we'd react?"

Ryan turned and focused on the control panel monitor. "What the—no, I'm not. But there are—"

"Yeah," Jack said. "Three armed men are moving our way."

Bill pointed at the video from camera nineteen. "There are more on camera nineteen. Look, more men on eighteen."

Ryan's heart pounded his sternum in what seemed like a long drum roll. "Tell me what weapons you see."

"Automatic rifles," Bill said.

"Grenade launchers and some RPGs," Jack said.

"This is no game, guys. We are under attack. Keep monitoring them while I call in our Huey Cobra." Ryan hit the speed dial for Rafer Jackson.

The phone rang once, twice, three times ...

Come on, Rafe, answer.

"Rafe, here. Is that you, Ryan?" He sounded sleepy.

"Rafe, we are coming under attack. Get the Huey here as quick as you can."

"I'm on my way." Rafe sounded wide awake now.

"Call me on the radio as soon as you take off. I'll give you their position. They're moving slowly from the outermost cameras toward the lab."

The sound of a car engine starting came through the phone.

"Ryan, I'll call you on the radio in about four minutes. Gotta go for now."

Ryan must notify everyone in the compound. The early risers might be awake. The others would be in bed. He opened a text that he would broadcast to everyone's cell.

The lab is coming under attack from a well-armed, unknown force. Stay inside your homes until further notice.

Rafe is on his way to the airport. The Huey Cobra will be here in about eight or nine minutes.

A reply came from Baker.

Lee's apartment is closest to the attackers.

Getting my M4 and moving to Lee's location.

Must hold them off until Huey arrives.

"Three guys are loading up RPGs on their launchers." Bill's voice.

"Keep track of the leading edge of the attackers and any attempt to shoot anything our way," Ryan said. "Let me know as soon as you have a rough count of the size of the force."

"I see what might be the back of the troops," Jack said. "If so, there are thirty-five to forty men."

"The Huey Cobra can take them out if we can hold them off until he arrives," Ryan said. "How fast are they moving?"

"They're being cautious," Bill said. "I'm not sure why, but that will help us. How long until that Cobra gets here?"

"About six or seven more minutes," Ryan said.

Jack spread his outstretched fingers of one hand over the map of the monitored area. "At the rate they're moving, that's about when they'll reach the front edge of the trees."

"There are around forty of them," Bill said. "They appear to be in two groups with slightly different uniforms. They are segregating by their uniforms."

"Segregating?" Ryan nodded toward Bill. "We'll take any advantage we can get at this point."

Bill grinned in return. "Hey, Ryan, do we get combat pay for this morning?"

"You guys certainly deserve it. Jack, keep updating us on when it looks like the first troops will reach the leading edge of the trees."

It grew quiet in the weather station room for the next few moments as all three men studied video from the security cameras.

The radio squawked, and Rafe's voice sounded over it. "Cobra one to the lab—I'm lifting off. Over target in two minutes."

"Lab to Cobra one—roger that. That's about when the shooting will start. Can you make an initial pass starting from the trees by the lab and moving eastward to the back of the trees?"

"Cobra one—will make pass as you directed, taking out closest attackers first. Tell Pierce there may not be any trees left when I'm finished."

"Lab here—that sounds good to me. No more hiding places for the bad guys. Gotta go shoot some guys aiming RPGs at us. Handing the radio to the security monitor, Bill."

Ryan gave Bill the radio mic. "You know Rafe. Just answer his questions. You have my cell number. Text me if you need to pass any info to me."

He pulled his Sig Sauer from his SOB holster, scurried out of the room, and ran down the hall toward the lobby entrance to the lab.

As he ran, visions ran through his mind— images of his apartment exploding as RPGs hit it. Meiling was inside, and his text message told her to stay there.

God, protect her. Help Rafe to get here in time. Enable us to stop the evil forces attacking us.

From the outside corner of the lobby, he could use the building as a shelter and yet see the nearest grove of trees where the attackers would gather to start shooting. That was over a hundred yards away. With only a handgun, could he hit the men or anything close to them to make them take cover at that distance?

Ryan stopped in the lobby, crept out the door, and moved to the corner of the building.

The sun had not risen yet, but the twilight was bright, certainly bright enough for the attackers to see their targets.

When Ryan peered around the corner, he saw nothing but the leading edge of the trees.

With a click, he loaded a shell into the chamber. But with only a fifteen-round magazine in his gun, he couldn't waste a single shot in his attempt to make the attackers seek shelter until the Cobra arrived.

A text message sounded its alert on his phone.

Attackers are about a minute away from edge of trees.

He acknowledged the text with a K.

Behind the apartments, to Ryan's right, Baker's short, muscular form darted from Jinghua's apartment toward Lee's, the closest apartment to the attackers.

It appeared that Baker had his M4.

Baker had no choice but to use the corner of Lee's apartment as cover, just as Ryan was doing with a corner of the lab lobby. But Baker would draw heavy fire that would hit Lee's place. If the attackers responded with an RPG, Lee might not survive.

With each step toward this confrontation, it had seemed that the possibilities grew more menacing.

Baker stopped in the gap between Jinghua's and Lee's apartments, looked Ryan's way, and waved.

Ryan waved back.

In the distance, the pulsating roar of the racing Huey Cobra came from the south.

Two men carrying RPG launchers appeared beside the nearest trees and lowered the launchers into firing position.

Chapter 15

6:30 a.m.

Ryan took a quick aim at the two men and fired a five-round volley.

The men appeared startled, and they jumped behind the two nearest trees.

Three more men appeared to the right. One had an RPG launcher.

The staccato cracking of Baker's M4 sounded, and shredded vegetation exploded into the air near the three newcomers.

One of the men went down.

Another of the three fired his automatic weapon.

A loud thwack near Ryan's head sent shards of concrete flying.

Some small debris stung Ryan's cheek and his right arm before he jumped back to cover.

Baker's shooting had stopped too. He had likely taken cover.

The door to Jinghua's apartment opened and she stood in the doorway.

The shooters could not see her yet.

But if she stepped out—Ryan waved her back in.

Jinghua obeyed.

He turned his focus back on the men in the trees.

The group of five had now grown to at least ten. Four had RPGs ready to fire.

To Ryan's right, the Cobra turned to make a pass beginning directly over the lab compound.

Baker's gun had gone silent. Was he hit?

The Huey's peculiar whirring noise and rapid staccato beat grew loud.

The men in the trees had turned all their attention to the Huey Cobra. But they looked confused.

They probably hadn't anticipated a military helicopter attacking them. It was a formidable weapon, even if it was antiquated by twenty-first-century standards. But did they recognize it?

Just as the men in the trees turned to run, Rafe hit the M129 40 mm grenade launcher. Grenades ripped through the sky overhead at seven grenades per second. One burst took out the entire left side of the trees for a distance Ryan couldn't determine due to the smoke.

The second burst took out the rest of the trees as the Cobra passed over Ryan.

The Cobra circled to the right and came back over the compound. This time Rafe had chosen the M134 Minigun. This six-barrel rotary machine gun sprayed the wooded area with bullets at one hundred per second. Rafe gave the attackers four hundred bullets.

A light breeze from the west cleared the smoke and dust from the targeted area, beginning with the leading edge of the trees. There, Ryan saw several bodies strewn across the plowed-up ground.

If anyone in the trees had survived, they would have been severely wounded or traumatized.

Baker! How could Ryan have forgotten him? He'd heard nothing from Baker since the M4's burst of fire that had hit some of the attackers.

Ryan sprinted across the parking area to Jinghua's apartment and slipped behind it to stay undercover while moving to Lee's apartment.

Standing against the compound's fence by Lee's apartment, Baker surveyed the damage. He glanced back at Ryan. "Checking up on me, bro?"

"Yeah. I hadn't heard anything, so—"

"I'm fine. But let's keep everyone in their apartments until we verify that no one else wants to continue the attack."

"You mean there are people that foolish?"

"You never know, bro. After getting hit that hard, some men go crazy with fear, and others go crazy with anger."

Ryan pointed to the northwest of the compound where Rafe was landing in a field. "And we'd be in those men's shoes if we didn't have that Cobra protecting us."

"Since they had RPGs, probably so," Baker said. "That's why we took the trouble of flying that snake out here from Oregon and stocking up on ammo." He paused and looked at Rafe getting out of the Huey Cobra. "Let's have a chat with Rafe. I'd like him to survey the area from the air before we go traipsing across it looking for survivors. Come on. Let's catch him before he gets too far from his bird."

They jogged toward Rafe.

He stopped and waited for them to reach him.

"Great job, Rafe," Baker said. "But we need to know if there are any left who might shoot if we start looking for survivors."

"So you want me to go back up and scan the area? There's another danger you need to be aware of."

"What's that?" Baker said.

The battlefield had grown quiet after the whine of the Huey's engine faded away. Now, Ryan heard the wailing of several sirens coming from the direction of Superior.

"I hear them, Rafe," Ryan said. "How many are there?"

"At least two fire trucks and enough police to make a SWAT team or two. The thing is, they've likely never seen anything like this in their entire careers. When they realize there was a war here, they will be as nervous as a long-tailed cat in a room full of rocking chairs. I'm afraid they might become that adage shoot first and ask questions later."

"Rafe, we don't even know who these people are. We don't know if any of them are alive. We have maybe three or four minutes before the cops arrive. So, what do you recommend?"

"I'll make a quick pass over the area and see if there are signs of life. The Huey in the air ought to tell them that we're Americans, and we were at war with some folks who were not patriotic Americans. Ryan, you want to come along and be another set of eyes."

"Sure. I'd love to."

"And leave me to face the cops?"

"If they try to arrest you, I could change their minds with a demo from the M129 grenade gun."

"Please don't. They might just shoot me and run."

"Baker, it will be much easier on us if they see me hovering over the area, and then you tell them what I'm doing. They might agree to help us comb the area, capture any survivors, and search the bodies to see if we can find out who was trying to kill us and take out the lab at the same time."

"Take Ryan and go, Rafe. I'll walk back to the compound and wait until you give the all-clear sign. I can use the time to broadcast a text message telling our people hunkered down in their apartments what's going on."

"Come on, Ryan." Rafe jogged back to the Huey with Ryan right behind him. "Climb in back and buckle in. We've got to survey the battlefield before the cops get here."

By the time Ryan got the door open and buckled in, the Huey's engine was screaming, and the blades had begun that wop, wop sound.

The bird tilted forward, leaped into the air, and raced to the area that had been covered with trees an hour ago.

When Ryan thought to put the headset on, Rafe was telling him he didn't see anything moving.

Ryan scanned the area to his right.

Rafe spun the Huey around in a one-eighty and started back over the battlefield.

Ryan saw no movement except for a gaggle of cop cars gathering at the head of the lab's driveway.

"Some men might be alive, but I don't think they could fight. We'll land near the cop cars and hope they realize our intent isn't malicious."

"Aren't our windows bulletproof?" Ryan said.

"Yes. But I'd rather not test them right now."

Rafe cozied up to the cops' cluster of cars and motioned that he was going to land.

One cop pointed at an open area fifty yards to the south.

Rafe nodded and proceeded to land there.

After he set the Huey down, the engine began its dying whine, and Rafe opened his door.

Ryan followed suit.

But when Ryan crawled out of the helicopter, a dozen cops scurried toward them with their guns drawn.

Chapter 16

7:15 a.m.

Ryan and Rafe climbed out of the Huey Cobra and headed toward the cops, who had slowed to a cautious walk.

"Hands on your heads!" The lead cop bellowed the words.

Ryan and Rafe complied but didn't reply.

The group of policemen moved closer. "Now, tell us what just went down out here," the big guy who appeared to be the leader of the cops said.

Ryan met the man's piercing glare. "You are all aware of Dr. Pierce's lab and our work here for the president's Marburg Pandemic response."

"Chopper Charlie, suppose you tell us how civilians use an attack helicopter for medical research."

"Rafe glanced at Ryan, then looked back at the cop. "How would the good folks of Superior, Colorado like it if the BSL-4 lab was breached, blown up, and some nasty pathogens wafted on the breeze through their little town?"

"You didn't answer my question."

The cop looked like he was working himself into a frenzy. Ryan needed to stop him before he exploded. "We were just attacked by an unidentified paramilitary group who were in the process of launching several RPGs into the lab when we hit them with our Cobra's RPG gun. When you showed up, we were scanning the area for survivors."

"It looks like you fought a war here," the big policeman said.

"We had a fierce firefight for a few minutes until the Huey Cobra arrived. But we need to identify the perpetrators. This war may not be over. They could be attacking the Marburg mAbs production facilities right now, and we don't even know who they are or whom they represent."

"Yes, officer," Rafe said. "Will you please help us look for survivors and help identify these people? There appear to be two groups with slightly different camouflage uniforms and different equipment."

"Who are we agreeing to help?"

Ryan released a big sigh. The cops were finally viewing him and Rafe as good guys ... or at least as non-threatening.

Baker appeared on the driveway, jogging toward them with his M4 slung over his shoulder.

"That's Radley Baker, ex-Special Forces. He pilots our Gulfstream G550. He was also in on the firefight."

"It sounds like you have your own paramilitary force too."

"Just the three of us," Ryan said.

"Just the three of you." The cop had returned to his sarcastic voice. "How long did it take you to ***denude*** our forest out here?"

Rafe grinned. "About five seconds."

A cop in the group of twelve whistled.

"If we weren't on your side, you would all have been meeting St. Peter at the gate," Rafe said. "That would have taken about two seconds using our M129."

The big policeman mumbled some choice expletives, clearly defining his thoughts about the situation.

Baker slowed to a walk as he approached them. "Hey, guys. If we don't make a pass through the battlefield area, a survivor could get up and start shooting. And it's not like they were carrying muskets. They had state-of-the-art military guns, automatics." He paused. "Officer, I wouldn't dillydally if I were you."

"Baker, did you tell everybody the coast was clear?" Ryan said.

"Yeah. But I told them to remain inside the compound and, if they heard any shooting, to go back to their apartments until we told them it was safe to come out."

The head cop looked frustrated, probably because he was losing control of the conversation. "Listen up, everybody. We are going to make a pass through the ***denuded forest***. We need to identify the paramilitary group that attacked the lab and take any survivors into custody. Some ambulances followed us out here. Make sure you disarm any wounded people before turning them over to the paramedics. Remember, these are likely trained military personnel, not your run-of-the-mill street punks. So, be careful. And Willis, tell the ambulance drivers to move their vehicles to our position."

Ryan waited until the policeman had finished giving instructions. "Officer, we should start here, from the back of the trees. That's where you will most likely find survivors. The Cobra hit the edge of the trees nearest the lab pretty hard. That's where they placed their RPG launchers."

"How many casualties do you think there might be?" The officer's gaze darted back and forth between Ryan and Baker.

"As many as forty," Baker said.

"Holy smoke!" one of the officers blurted out.

"I don't think so," Ryan said. "Where these guys are going, the smoke won't be holy."

Rafe pointed at the Huey about fifty yards away. "Just in case, I'm guarding my bird until this is all over."

"Willis," the big officer called out. "Tell the ambulance drivers to call for some more help. We could have as many as forty bodies to deal with."

"Do you two want to help us search through the, uh—"

"The ***denuded forest***?" Baker said.

"Better to have a denuded forest than a denuded BSL-4 lab." Ryan grinned. "We'd be glad to help."

"Listen up, men. All of you except Willis line up across the damaged area. We will make a pass through it, counting the dead bodies, searching them for any identification, and confiscating weapons. If you find a survivor, call the paramedics and wait there until they arrive."

As they moved down the path of destruction, some trees still stood but had their lower limbs stripped bare. The M129's grenades had mowed down or ripped up all other vegetation.

Ryan and Baker had taken the left side of the area beside the sergeant.

At the sergeant's command, the group began a cautious advance into the area of death and destruction.

Ryan stopped to examine the first body he encountered. The man had carried an M4. The fatigues looked like American military issue but had no insignia of rank. But there was a logo Ryan had only seen once or twice in news articles. The logo included the letters GTI, which stood for Global Threat Initiative, a radical population-control group responsible for several terrorist attacks worldwide.

Baker had stopped beside another body.

"Baker, what've you got?"

"Looks like an American with American weapons and a GTI patch. If this isn't some false flag operation, we have a terrorist attack by people who would like our lab to fail."

"My guy's Caucasian," Ryan said.

"Mine too."

A trooper on the far-right side called out to the sergeant. "Sarge, every casualty we've found over here is Chinese. But they had GTI patches. Their weapons are not American. Something's not right."

Baker ambled over to the man who was about thirty yards away. “Let me see the weapon you found.”

Even from this distance, Ryan could see the gun was not American.

“This is what the Iranians and North Koreans use,” Baker said. “Now it’s starting to make sense.” Baker jogged back to his spot on the left side and resumed the search without telling Ryan what made sense.

Ryan found another body, a Caucasian, and searched the uniform. He felt an object inside the lower right side of the coat.

He eventually found the hidden opening and pulled out a thin leather wallet. When he opened it, a driver’s license picture stared back at Ryan. “Hey, sergeant. I just struck gold over here. I’ve got a wallet with ID in it.”

The big sergeant hurried over and looked at the ID. “Davis!”

A man to their right jogged over. “What’s up, sarge?”

“We have our first ID. Run it for me. Let’s see who this guy is.”

The sergeant placed a marker on the body, and they continued moving forward in their search.

In about five minutes, Davis returned. “You’re not gonna believe this, sarge. This guy is an FBI agent.”

“I can believe it,” Baker said.

Ryan nodded. “Me too. “They’ve been allied with the medical bureaucrats against my wife, Meiling, since the beginning of the pandemic.”

The sergeant’s eyebrows rose. “Your wife is Meiling Chen-Adams?”

Ryan nodded again. “We tried to tell you the work at this lab supports President Warrington’s Marburg response.”

“Maybe this is beginning to make a little sense now,” the sergeant said. “By the way, I’m Officer Barry. You’re Ryan Adams.” He turned to Baker. “Who are you?”

"I'm Radley Baker, Ex-Special Forces. Now I fly the lab personnel around in my Gulfstream."

"And the other guy's an attack helicopter pilot. That's quite a group you've assembled."

Ryan nodded. He was not going to tell Sergeant Barry about the rest of the group, including the Chief Scientist from the Wuhan Institute of Virology and two of his former employees.

"We're almost done," Barry said. "Let's wrap up the search and then put our heads together to see what this attack was about."

The body count had reached twenty-nine by the time they reached the area nearest the compound where the men with RPG launchers had congregated.

An officer to their right cursed. "Sarge, you're not going to believe this. They had ten RPGs loaded and ready to shoot."

"Yeah," Baker said. "Our Huey Cobra arrived with no time to spare. If Rafe had arrived thirty seconds later, the lab would have been hit and some of our people killed. Who knows what pathogens might have escaped biosafety containment?"

Ryan glanced at the compound a hundred yards ahead.

Meiling stood inside the gate, studying them.

"Baker, Meiling's at the gate. I need to check in with her. I'll be back."

"Go check in, dude. I've heard it's a rather pleasant experience." Baker grinned and waved him on toward Meiling.

Ryan jogged to the gate.

Meiling had opened it for him by the time he arrived. She gave him a bear hug strong enough to have come from a man, and then she kissed him. "I heard what sounded like a war. I feared for you even more than when we fought the PLA in Wuhan."

"We're all okay, sweetheart."

"Thank God that you are. What did you find out about the attack?"

"Well, about half of the attackers are Chinese. The other half, we're not sure about. But one of them had ID on him. He was an FBI agent. All of them had GTI patches on their uniforms."

"GTI, the terrorist group that wants to depopulate the planet?"

"Yes. But we think this is a false flag attack. I believe we're looking at a team consisting of two groups, PLA soldiers already in the U.S. and rogue FBI affiliated with the medical bureaucrats. They were trying to shut down both you and the president's Marburg response."

"That's what I was afraid of, Ryan. Even though this attack failed, they could still shut down the Marburg response if they took out the manufacturing plants, MABS International and ProtSyn. We've got to warn them and protect them."

"But we've got to continue to protect the lab too."

"I know," Meiling said. "We should have a meeting of our lab staff to decide what we're going to do, and that must happen right now. We might have only minutes until this corrupt crew decides it needs to hit MABS and ProtSyn."

Chapter 17

8:10 a.m.

While Meiling and Ryan discussed the security problem at ProtSyn and MABS, Baker jogged up to the gate.

Meiling waved him toward her and Ryan. "Baker, I have a big concern for the security of the two manufacturing plants in Minnesota. We need to meet immediately to plan how we are going to protect them."

"I was thinking along the same line," Baker said. "These guys failed here with the lab, so they need another approach to take down Warrington's Marburg strategy."

Sergeant Barry strode to the gate shortly after Baker arrived.

Baker turned toward the big sergeant. "It seems we have another security problem. We believe this motley crew may have planned something else for today at the Marburg mAbs manufacturing plants in Minnesota. How would you protect them?"

"Minnesota ... well, you have two choices, the state or the federal government. It seems Dr. Chen-Adams has the ear of the president. I'd start there. But changing the subject—we will be here for a few hours hauling away bodies and compiling information. I want you two, Baker and Ryan, to call me if you plan to leave the compound. Do not disappear on me." He gave Baker a card with his cell number on it. "By the way, we found one survivor."

Baker looked up from the card in his hand. "Was he from the FBI group or the Chinese?"

"FBI. Well, he's Caucasian. Maybe he will tell us who put him up to this attack."

"Don't count on it," Baker said. "That might cost him his life."

"If he doesn't talk, it might cost him life in prison," Barry said.

"If he talks, let us know," Ryan said. "That might tell us what we need to secure."

"Maybe," Barry said. "He's barely conscious. They took him to the trauma center at Denver Health. It may be a while before we can question him."

"Like Ryan said, let us know if you learn anything that helps us," Baker said.

Barry nodded, then turned and strode away toward the gruesome work on the battlefield.

Baker pulled out his phone. "I'm calling Rafe. He needs to be at this meeting." He keyed in Rafe's number.

"Yeah, it's Baker ... move the Huey to the other side of the lab, away from all the people and activity, then meet us in the conference room in about five minutes ... Yes, it's that important." Baker ended the call.

Meiling started the meeting when Rafe entered the conference room at 8:20 a.m. "We need to call MABS International and ProtSyn and warn them."

"Do you want to call them before we have a plan or suggestions to secure their labs?" Ryan said.

"They have limited security at their plants," Meiling said. "Rafe, can you and the Huey help?"

Rafe shook his head. "It's over seven hundred miles to Minneapolis. The Huey's range is only about three hundred and fifty miles. At one hundred forty miles per hour with one fuel stop, it would take me four hours to get there. If we're right about the threat, using the Huey is not feasible."

"You're right, Rafe," Baker said. "Besides, the two facilities, MABS in Minneapolis and ProtSyn in Rochester, are ninety miles apart. We need to protect them against simultaneous attacks. These guys couldn't pull off attacks several hours apart. We'd be onto them after the first attack."

Meiling hooked an arm around Ryan's waist. "So what are we going to do?"

"We really only have one option," Baker said. "The one Barry mentioned. Use the federal government. To me, that means the Air Guard in Minnesota. They have F-16s."

"Refresh my mind, bro," Rafe said. "What's an F-16 got for armament?"

"They've got more than adequate armament—MK82 five-hundred-pound bombs, air-to-ground missiles, and a twenty-millimeter Vulcan cannon that shoots eight-inch shells at a hundred rounds per second. They can use armor-penetrating or explosive shells. The question is, which weapons can we use near a manufacturing plant?"

"Where are the air guards located?" Ryan asked.

"The F-16s are in Duluth," Baker said. "They can fly at over one thousand miles per hour. It would take maybe ten minutes from notification to an attack on a target in Minneapolis. Maybe a minute more to Rochester."

Baker paused. "How do we get authorization to use the Air Guard? Do we call the governor of Wisconsin or the president?"

Meiling reached for the conference room phone. "I'm going to call MABS International and ProtSyn now. They need to alert their security about the danger and to know what we're working on to protect them."

She placed the call and took the phone to the far side of the table, away from the team's conversation.

"We don't know the governor of Minnesota and, besides, he may have sided with the Colorado AG against Meiling," Ryan said. "The case has been in the national news."

"Meiling and the president are buds," Baker said. "We should call Warrington, and Meiling should make the call."

Meiling hung up the conference room phone.

"Well," Ryan said. "What was their reaction?"

"Panic. Their security is not up for this kind of a fight."

"Meiling," Baker said. "While you were on the phone, we nominated you to call President Warrington to activate the Air Guard for us."

"But we need to go through Colonel West," Meiling said. "Baker, you understand the military nuances better than I do. You should make the call."

"Okay. But only if we turn on the speaker and you participate, Meiling."

Baker took the conference room phone, turned on the speaker, and keyed in Colonel West's number.

"Colonel West here. Is this Meiling?"

"This is Baker. West, we have the whole team in the conference room. We held off a major attack against the lab today, but we need—"

"Define major attack, Baker." West's voice turned icy.

"Forty trained men with automatic weapons and a bevy of RPGs."

"Is everyone okay?"

"Thanks to the Huey Cobra. But we believe there's a part two to this battle, and we need the president's help with what the opponents to our Marburg response are about to do."

"I need to make sure POTUS is needed before calling him. What is this predicted part two, Baker?"

Baker explained the threat to both MABS International and ProtSyn. "The only solution we see is to get help from the Air Guards. Duluth has F-16s that, under the right conditions, could destroy the attackers in seconds."

"And what are those conditions?" West asked.

"We will need continuous surveillance of both manufacturing plants. F-16s from Duluth could be at either location in ten minutes. But if we kept those birds circling over the vicinity, they could strike in a minute or two. However, I think we can only use the F-16s if it's still light. This time of year, it gets too dark at about 9:30 p.m."

"Thanks, Baker," West said. "I believe you're right in wanting to use F-16s. We can't let these bureaucratic terrorists destroy the facilities we use to fight the—"

"Hold it for a second, West." Baker's cell had sounded the alarm for an incoming message. "I'm getting a message from an observer at the MABS plant."

Baker studied the display on his phone.

"Not good. Police observers near the MABS plant say that a road crew and a group of power line workers are congregating along a street about two hundred yards from the MABS plant's fence. They can strike quickly from that location."

"Maybe they really are doing roadwork," West said.

"Right. And I'm really just planning a joy ride for some F-16 pilot." Baker blew out his frustration in a sharp blast of air.

Meiling's cell rang. "I'd better take this call. It's from ProtSyn at Rochester."

The conference room was buzzing with chatter now.

Meiling stood and walked to a quieter corner of the room. "This is Meiling ... Yes ... Are you sure they are road workers ... How many are there ... Thanks ... We are working the problem right now with our contact in D.C." She ended the call.

"Don't tell me, Meiling," Baker said. "Let me guess. ProtSyn has a dozen or so road workers outside their manufacturing plant."

"That's right." Meiling came back to the table and slid her cell into her pocket.

"What are the odds of that," Ryan said. "Crews doing road maintenance simultaneously at the only two Marburg treatment manufacturing plants in the USA. Coincidence? I don't think so."

Chapter 18

9:00 a.m. lab conference room

A thought jolted Baker out of the security of his plan to crush the attackers with F-16's armament. "What do we do if the attackers wait for darkness before attacking the plants?"

Ryan looked across the table at Baker. "Can the infrared homing device on the missile target a human body or a small group of men so we can shoot and hit them in the dark?"

"In theory, it can," Baker said. "But it was designed to be effective against tactical targets like armored vehicles, air defense sites, ships, and ground vehicles."

Rafe's focus darted back and forth between Ryan and Baker. "So we're not certain we can hit some men running across a field in the dark?"

"No. We aren't certain." Baker's reply came wrapped in the soft voice of resignation.

Ryan caught Baker's gaze. "But maybe there is a way to force the attack to happen before dark."

"What have you got in that meteorological mind of yours, Ryan?" Baker gave him a dubious smile.

"These dudes won't be willing to give up their mission just because they detect something like a cop car approaching them, even if the cops seem interested in them. But suppose the cop parked out of sight and used one of those 50-Watt megaphones to tell them to leave because the city is conducting a disaster-response exercise in the area."

Rafe folded his hands on the table. "If the cops were close enough, the bad dudes would kill the cops and then attack the factory."

Ryan nodded. "You can hear those megaphones for a half mile or more. So, if the cops were too far away to kill, and there were too many of them, what would the attackers do?"

"No doubt about it," Baker said. "They'd attack right then before the police could stop them."

"I agree," Rafe said. "They'd attack. He paused. "But I think I should get a 50-Watt phone for my Huey. It might come in handy."

Baker grinned. "Don't you mean ***my*** Huey?"

Rafe nodded slowly. But there's a love affair growing fast between her and me."

Ryan pounded his fist on the table. "Then that's the backup plan. If they haven't attacked by 9:00 p.m., we force the attack using the cops. The sun sets in Minneapolis at 9:00 p.m. today. It gets dark around 9:35. Things should move quickly after the cops tell the road workers to leave."

Meiling gave Ryan a questioning glance. "In case our plan fails to get the attackers, shouldn't we send police into the factory now to protect the workers?"

Ryan met her gaze and shook his head. "No, Meiling. Our plan works because of the element of surprise. We can wipe them all out in a second or two. If they abort the attack because they see police going into the factory, we may never catch them. And we don't want to risk the lives of policemen. They aren't trained to combat highly trained special forces."

"Being highly trained doesn't matter if the police overwhelmingly outnumber the bad guys," Baker said.

"Maybe we should describe the scenario and let the police work out the details," Ryan said.

"We need to get this mission rolling," West said. "I'll call President Warrington and try to get him on a conference call with us. But realize this; he won't authorize F-16s to blow a road-work crew to kingdom come unless he has verified that they are attacking our production plants."

Baker shook his head. "That means we can't hit them until they attack. We'd better have those F-16s circling about ten miles away. They could reach the target in about forty-five seconds. That would be sufficient to stop attackers who have to traverse a two-hundred-yard field and then scale or cut through a fence topped with barbwire to gain access to the plant."

"And we can't have an F-16 shooting missiles at targets only thirty yards from the buildings," Ryan said.

"I'm not so sure about that, Ryan," West said. "These are highly accurate missiles, and we can use a couple of different warheads. We need the contact-fuse-based warheads for this mission and probably the smaller missile, the one weighing a hundred twenty-five pounds."

"Then let's get the distance from the fences to the buildings for both facilities," Baker said. "Meiling, you call ProtSyn, and I'll take MABS."

After two short phone conversations, they had determined that the distance from the fence to the buildings was about thirty yards for both facilities.

"If they start the assault before dark, we can stop them with an air attack after we get approval from the president and authorization for the Air Guard to carry out the mission."

"I would advise you to have the two companies clear any employees from the part of the buildings where the missiles will land," West said. "If we can't hit the attackers before they reach the fence, the buildings will be within the kill radius of the warhead. The walls will experience some damage."

"I will call MABS International and ProtSyn and let them know," Meiling said.

"Then it's time for me to bring the president into this discussion," Colonel West said. "His schedule says he's in the Oval Office and currently between meetings. Hang on for a minute while I get him."

"Remember, West," Baker said. "He doesn't know about the attack on the lab this morning, the outcome, or what we found."

"Got it. Hang on for a few minutes while I brief him and bring him into the conference call."

It grew quiet in the conference room. Ryan could hear the clock on the wall ticking—ticking toward attacks that would succeed if Warrington did not act quickly enough.

"This is President Warrington. Tell me about the attack on the lab that West mentioned."

"This is Baker, Mr. President. We were attacked early this morning by a team of forty men disguised as GTI members. Twenty PLA soldiers and twenty FBI agents made the assault. Fortunately, Rafer Jackson flew our Huey Cobra to the lab and took them out just as they prepared to launch a dozen RPGs into the lab building."

"Were any of our people hurt?"

"No, Mr. President. But we came near to being wiped out and the lab destroyed."

"Were there any survivors among the attackers?"

"Yes. One verified FBI agent survived. He has not recovered sufficiently to question him. But after those ordering the attack realized it had failed, they immediately sent a group of men disguised as road and power-line workers to streets adjacent to the MABS International plant in Minneapolis and ProtSyn's plant in Rochester. If we do not stop them, they could bring our Marburg response to a halt with no good alternative available."

"Except the ***crappy vaccines*** Phisher and some other big pharmaceutical companies are working on." Meiling's words dripped with disdain.

Ryan tried to get his hand near her mouth to stop the verbal explosion that might prejudice the president against their proposed method of stopping the attacks.

Meiling pushed his hand away. "And I would bet big money that the CCP, the WHO, maybe our CDC, and our own FBI are in on this attempt to take over the handling of the Marburg Pandemic. If they destroy the mAbs and killer protein factories, that is treason, and they have already committed it once today by attacking our lab."

"I appreciate your zeal for our cause, Meiling. But what are you asking me to do?"

"This is Baker, Mr. President. The attacks could begin at any moment. We are in imminent danger of losing both production facilities. We need support from the Minneapolis Air Guard. Their F-16s are equipped with missiles and twenty-millimeter cannons that could wipe out the attackers in a few seconds. The police or ground troops couldn't do that, nor could they respond quickly enough. Sir, will you activate the Air Guard to stop the attackers?"

"Before I order our military to kill a bunch of men, I must know that they are, in fact, going to attack."

"We won't know that, sir, until they move against the plant. In both cases, Minneapolis and Rochester, the men must cross open fields nearly two hundred yards wide, giving us only about forty seconds to take them out. If we keep F-16s in the air ten miles away until the danger has been eliminated, we can strike with an air-to-ground missile in approximately forty seconds."

"We cannot lose those manufacturing plants, Baker. Will you stay on the line with me while I call Governor Hatcher?"

"Like you said, sir, we can't lose those plants. I would suggest that you call the Air Guard commander with the orders and then notify the Minnesota Governor. I'm sure he will understand. The clock is ticking, Mr. President. And we can't let it get too late, or darkness will jeopardize our plan to use F-16s. If the attackers appear to be waiting on darkness, we must force them to attack."

"And how pray tell would you propose to do that, Baker?"

"That's where your call to Governor Hatcher comes in," Baker said. "He could order police to monitor the situation while hidden a safe distance away."

Baker paused. "At sunset, police, masquerading as city officials, could order the road crews to leave because the street will be used in a disaster-response exercise. If they don't attack, then they lose their opportunity. If they leave instead of attacking, police could follow them, surround them with a large force, and arrest them. But, sir, they will not leave when ordered to do so. I'm confident they will attempt to attack the factories."

President Warrington sighed long and loud into the phone. "Okay. I am calling General Meyer, Commander of the 148th Fighter Wing, federalizing his wing and ordering him to carry out what Baker described. And you will help negotiate the details of this mission, Baker. That may require a few changes based upon General Meyer's experience."

"Yes, sir," Baker replied. "Uh, Mr. President, if you patch me in, you will be bringing in our entire team here in the conference room."

"Tell the rest of them to be quiet, especially Meiling. I understand why she's angry, but her anger will not help to get the Air Guard fighters in the air so we can stop those ***crappy vaccines***."

Ryan locked gazes with Meiling.

She glared at him, but she nodded ... with pursed lips.

"She heard, Mr. President," Ryan said.

"Good. I am calling General Meyer now."

Chapter 19

10:00 a.m. lab conference room

Unless he acted swiftly, the situation in Minnesota could end in the tortuous deaths of millions of people from the modified virus.

President Warrington put the conference call with the lab on hold while he called General Meyer, Commander of the 148th Fighter Wing of the Minnesota Air guard.

"148th Fighter Wing, General Meyer here."

"General Meyer, this is President Warrington. We have a national and possibly international crisis brewing in Minnesota as we speak. I need the immediate support of your wing to end this threat."

"Mr. President," he paused. "I called the wing to alert status. Please give me the specifics on how we can help."

"General Meyer, I am bringing you into a conference call with me and the medical team working with Dr. Meiling Chen-Adams in Colorado. They have veteran pilots on that team who can fill you in on the details of this mission."

Warrington returned to the conference call. "This is President Warrington. I have General Meyer on the line."

"General Meyer, here. I have put my fighter wing on alert. Please tell me why that was necessary."

"Baker," the president said. "Please give the details of this threat to General Meyer, including our plan to end the threat."

Baker explained the situation in Rochester and Minneapolis, including what was at stake if the attackers were not prevented from destroying or incapacitating the manufacturing plants.

"This is not what I anticipated on a lazy summer day. Gentlemen and ladies, I am replacing the air-to-air missiles on my fighters with air-to-ground Maverick H missiles that use contact fuses. We will do this on four F-16s. We can continuously keep two in the air, one circling near each location until the threat is neutralized."

"What about communications to support this?" Baker asked.

"An officer on my staff, Captain Towry, will assist me. Based on Baker's description of the police involvement, the captain is setting up a hotline between the police in these two cities and the 148th Fighter Wing. We will attack when the police see the assault starting."

General Meyer paused. "We need about fifteen minutes to swap out the missiles and ten minutes more for our birds to reach their holding positions."

"These Maverick missiles are AGM 65s, right, sir?" Baker asked.

"Yes. They will easily take out a cluster of a dozen men. The batteries on the F-16s have three missiles each, and we have two batteries on this bird. If you want to see an impressive demo of this missile, I will send you a link to a YouTube video from training at a firing range. I believe you will be pleased."

"Please do, sir," Baker said. "We'll be praying your birds are in position before these dudes decide to attack."

"They should be in position in twenty-five minutes." The general continued. "President Warrington, who do I contact when the threat has been neutralized."

"You should contact Colonel West. He reports directly to me," President Warrington said. "In a few minutes, I'll give you his number when I send you and Governor Hatcher a written copy of the activation orders. Are there any questions before I let you go to prepare your fighters for the mission?"

"I have a question for General Meyer," Baker said. "Under cover of darkness, can the Maverick AGM 65s infrared homing device target a human body or a small group of men?"

"Mr. Baker, rather than wandering into classified information, suffice it to say that your backup plan will work fine if we see the attackers waiting for darkness."

"The stakes are high, General Meyer. Our prayers are with you as you take on this mission." President Warrington ended the call.

***

Noon Eastern Time, secure conference room, Phisher Pharmaceuticals Headquarters, East Manhattan

No news, in this case, was bad news for Abe Borland. Maybe the upcoming meeting could rectify that situation.

Abe Borland locked the door to his office at the Phisher Pharmaceuticals headquarters and logged in to his VPN. He initiated the video conference with CDC Chief Operating Officer Dr. Marshall McDowell, General Liu Kuo of the People's Liberation Army, and FBI Deputy Director Harold Stein.

Harold was the last person to join the meeting. His face did not hold a good-news look.

Abe opened the meeting. "Good afternoon. I say that with a bit of trepidation. I have received no news from the lab assault team. It's not a good sign. Have any of you heard anything?"

Harold Stein blew out a blast of apparent frustration. "Yes. One of my men is in a hospital in Denver. He's in serious condition, but it looks like he will make it."

Marsh McDowell shook his large head that hung from a skinny, inadequate neck. "How in the world did you get that information? No one could trace him back to you or the FBI."

This was concerning, very concerning. "Who called you, Harold?"

Harold blew out another blast of air. "Police from Superior, Colorado. They found the fool because he tried hiding his ID inside his GTI uniform."

"What did you tell them?"

"I said he was under investigation for cooperating with a known terrorist group. They seemed satisfied with that answer. I'll create a paper trail to support what I told them."

"But did they ask more questions?"

"Yes, Abe, but nothing that should concern us."

"But it does concern us, all of us in this room. Why did the other FBI agents leave him behind?"

A pained expression distorted Harold's face. "They didn't. The others are all headed to the morgue."

Chaos broke out in the video meeting.

"What?"

"What"?

"How?"

"Where are my PLA officers?" General Kuo bellowed, nearly frothing at the mouth.

Harold took a deep breath, and Abe filled the meeting screen with Harold's camera view.

"General, all of your men were killed."

Chinese words flew from Kuo's mouth. The look on his face and the intensity of his voice said the man was cursing.

Abe would have cursed along with him—especially cursing that idiot of an FBI agent who carried his ID while on a highly illegal mission—but Abe's primary need now was not venting but preventing anyone from connecting the assault on Pierce's lab to anyone in this meeting.

"How could anyone affiliated with that lab kill an army of forty trained men?"

"You're not going to believe this," Harold said. "They have a Huey Cobra, an attack chopper from the Vietnam Era, a chopper still used by several armies today. The Sheriff from Superior said it was a gruesome sight. Our men never had a chance. According to what I was told, they were all killed in less than ten seconds ... except for one worrisome dufus."

"In light of that news, I assume that part two of our plan is in progress," Marsh said. "We need it now more than ever if we're going to wrest control of the pandemic response from Dr. Meiling Chen-Adams and that crew of misfits she has collected at Pierce's lab."

"Yes, part two is underway," Harold said. "We have a team of twelve special-forces-trained FBI agents at both factory locations. They are waiting for my signal to attack. And I am waiting for darkness to send them in."

"Waiting?" Abe said. "I assume they are well hidden."

"Hidden in plain sight," Harold said. "They are disguised as road workers. And the Huey Cobra is too far away to protect the factories. They will be destroyed, leaving the pharmaceutical companies, especially Phisher, as the president's only option for stopping this pandemic."

Chapter 20

6:45 p.m. Central time, the lab conference room

Meiling scanned the faces around the large conference room table. Ming sat beside Robert, eyes focused on the flatscreen monitor on the wall. The monitor displayed the streamed video from the MABS International security camera. The camera faced outward toward the street where, two hundred yards away, a road crew milled lazily around three trucks.

Beside Robert, Buck and Jinghua sat. If the position of their arms were any indication, they were holding hands under the table.

Jinghua, perhaps the loneliest of the four people from Wuhan, now had the undivided attention of Buck McKinney. On her other side, she had the fatherly care of Dr. Li, who had become simply Lee, as the caring heart underneath the old Communist shell was revealed by the work of Jesus in the old Maoist's heart.

Meiling leaned against Ryan's shoulder.

On Ryan's other side, his veteran friend, Rafer Jackson, tapped a finger on the table as he watched the video monitor. Baker sat beside Rafe. Baker's wife, Shauna, had decided the imminent event was not something her three-year-old twins should see. She had opted to keep them in her and Baker's apartment until the event was over.

Baker's cell rang, and he answered. "Baker here ... Hello, Sergeant Barry. What's up? ... In that case, I'll turn on my speakerphone. The entire team at Dr. Pierce's lab is here with me in our conference room."

He set the cell on the table. “Now, what were you saying about the wounded FBI agent in the lab attack this morning?”

“The man woke up, and we explained to him that his actions had met the legal definition of treason,” Barry said. “He had acted with intent to betray the United States by attempting to stop the pandemic response ordered by the president to save American lives. And we had more than the required two witnesses to validate his crime.”

“What was his response to that?”

“He started cooperating and had begun to answer some questions when the doctor came in and said we needed to let him rest for a while. We went out of the room to the hallway, where we ran into two FBI agents who were anxious to talk to the guy.”

“I’ll bet they were anxious,” Baker said. “They might be involved in the conspiracy against our lab and the president’s policies.”

“At this point, we don’t know if they represented the good guys at the bureau or those who have sold their souls to the devil.”

“Sergeant Barry, that’s why we must proceed with caution in dealing with the FBI. They could be—”

Rapid movement on the monitor drew everyone’s attention. Some of the faux road workers stared down the street toward the city.

“Barry, we’re watching live video of a possible target for another attack, and something is happening now. I’ll call you back in a bit.” Baker ended the call.

“They’re listening to the cops’ megaphone,” Ryan said.

“Yeah,” Baker said. “And it looks like it’s forcing them to attack now.”

Meiling shuddered as she saw the men pulling weapons and other equipment from the trucks.

The group of twelve scurried across the field toward the fence protecting the MABS International buildings.

The leader of the pack had almost reached the fence when he stopped and looked into the sky.

Smoke or dust exploded onto the screen, filling it and obscuring the view of the men and the field.

Two more pulses of smoke and dust burst onto the display before the screen went dark.

Rafe started whistling some vaguely familiar tune, and Baker joined him.

"Ryan, what are they—"

"It's the Air Force song, Wild Blue Yonder. May God have mercy on their souls because those twelve men are now in His presence, and I wouldn't want to be in their shoes."

***

7:50 p.m. Eastern time, secure conference room at Phisher Pharmaceuticals headquarters

Abe Borland, Marshall McDowell, and General Liu Kuo sat around a small table in the secure conference room at Phisher Pharmaceuticals in Manhattan.

Using one of his trusted contacts, Abe had found an FBI agent, Kyle Wagner, who was not loyal to Harold Stein, one who planned to resign after this job was done.

Kyle had hidden near the ProtSyn factory in Rochester, Minnesota, and Abe had him on a secure call.

"Mr. Borland, it appears the team just got the signal to attack from Stein. I'll leave my phone on for as long as I can."

A deep roar saturated the speaker.

The roar turned to a savage ripping sound.

"What the—"

The call went silent.

Abe sat staring at the conference table in disbelief.

General Kuo was the first to speak. "A jet aircraft took them all out, including your Mr. Kyle Wagner. I am certain because it is not the first time I have heard an air attack over a voice connection."

"General, if you are correct, it's a certainty that the dead men will be connected to Harold Stein," Marsh said. "They all work for him. They were his hand-picked undercover agents. If they run fingerprints, that will confirm it."

"But that's as far as we can let the linkage go," Abe said. "We must not allow them to associate us with Harold. He only came to Phisher's facilities once. We can explain that visit if necessary. And all phone calls with him have been on our secure phones."

"After losing forty-four FBI agents in a few days, Harold has to be as nervous as a cat," Marsh said. "There are forty-four chances to connect him to the attacks which President Warrington will brand as treason."

They could not overlook the possibility that Harold, if cornered, would strike a deal with the DOJ predicated on him disclosing all those involved in this conspiracy to derail President Warrington's Marburg response. That meant the men in this room had only one option.

"We've got to eliminate Stein before the DOJ takes him into custody," Abe said.

"Tomorrow, if not sooner," Marsh said.

Abe studied General Kuo's face for a moment. "General, you can always escape back to China. Marsh and I have no such option. So, will you carry out the execution?"

"If I do nothing, I can still go back to China. The stakes are much higher for you and Marsh McDowell. So, one of you should oversee this delicate matter."

Abe turned to Marsh. "You have implemented policies that have killed thousands. One more surely won't matter."

"My policies only did what was necessary."

"This ***is*** necessary, Marsh."

"Then why don't you inject him with one of your ***safe and effective*** jabs, Abe? How about the one associated with the sudden death syndrome?"

Abe took a calming breath. "We must not overreact from one small obstacle. And we must not turn on each other." He paused. "Why don't we invite Harold to a meeting in a secure location not associated with our businesses?"

Marsh's eyebrows rose. "And then make sure he doesn't get there safely?"

"That I ***can*** help with." General Kuo displayed his crooked smile. "Will a sniper be an appropriate method to dispense with Mr. Stein?"

"See, gentlemen," Abe said. "There is no need for panic if we just cooperate and use our collective intelligence. We will call Harold on a secure phone and tell him about the meeting at a rented corporate SCIF on Long Island. We will justify using a SCIF because of the importance of security for this meeting. The place I am considering has an open, ground-level parking lot lined by a grove of trees on one side. It's a perfect spot for sniping."

"Abe, who are we going to blame this assassination on?" Marsh said.

"Yes, we must have a plausible—what do Americans call it—scapegoat," Kuo said.

"We'll blame it on the FBI field agents who retaliated for Harold Stein getting forty-four agents killed by his stupidity."

"You do realize," Kuo said, "you are implying that we are stupid too, do you not?"

"General, we are doubly stupid. As a government-affiliated lab, Dr. Chen-Adams's team would need protection. We failed to comprehend that this small group could only be protected by powerful weapons, most likely from the air. They used an attack helicopter and the U.S. Air Force."

Abe paused. "I'll call Stein later this evening."

Marsh leaned back in his chair. "But that still leaves us with no way to remove Meiling Chen-Adams and company from controlling the president's Marburg response."

"Correction," Abe said. "It leaves us with no violent way to remove them. That means we must resort to legal maneuvers. I'm sure a young doctor fresh from China made some mistakes on her furious run down the dangerous path she chose. We need to uncover them and perhaps, have Congress grill her."

"But we are in the minority in both houses of Congress, Abe. We own no committee chairs."

"But our people on the committees still get to ask questions. And if they ask the right ones, the ones we have researched in advance, the good doctor could find herself and her team members guilty of multiple felonies. That is the kind of scandal that the media savors. They will spread it for us."

"Still, it's not a sure thing, Abe," Marsh said.

"Nothing in life is a sure thing, Marsh. You've got to make things happen."

General Kuo smiled. "He is correct. You must seize control and use your power to make things happen, or you cannot make any progress in this world."

Chapter 21

07:05 a.m., two days later

Meiling's eyes opened reluctantly. The sound that had roused her was her cell phone ringing.

"Meiling, are you going to answer it?" Ryan sat up in bed and prepared to reach for her phone. "Are you having morning sickness?"

"No. I'm over that. I'm just tired, sweetheart."

"So you're sleeping for two? I know you're eating for two."

"And I have a baby bump now. Well, sort of."

The annoying ring continued.

"I'll answer my phone. Since we're both awake now, I'll share it with you." She pressed the speaker phone. "Hello."

"Harold Stein is dead, and that wounded FBI" guy—"

"Slow down, Baker. We just woke up. I have Ryan on too. Did you say Stein is dead?"

"Yeah. I just got a call from that Superior Police officer, Sergeant Barry. He said somebody assassinated Stein, the deputy FBI director. Sniped him on Long Island."

"Then you started to say something about the wounded FBI agent. Is he okay?" Ryan asked.

"That's a matter of opinion. The Superior Police just got a writ of *habeas corpus* from a lawyer representing the FBI."

Ryan pushed a lock of hair from his eye. "So the FBI is trying to get custody of one of their own who tried to attack us?"

"We cannot let them have him." Meiling grabbed her cell, sat up on the bed, and swung her legs over the side.

"They might kill him so he cannot incriminate others in the bureau who know about the attacks on our team."

"Right. Their deputy director was in on the attempt to kill us. Who knows if there's anyone in that organization we can trust."

"Did Sergeant Barry have any other news for us?" Ryan said.

"Yeah. We're not positive yet, but the guy who carried his ID and the survivor appear to have worked directly for Harold Stein."

Meiling stood beside the bed. "The FBI would not have decided to attack us without some other group providing the motivation."

"Let's see," Ryan said. "There's the healthcare bureaucrats, big pharma—"

"You can stop right there," Baker said. "I think you've covered all the bases. We don't know exactly who the bad actors are within those two groups. That's all I had," Baker said. "Guess I'll let you two lazy bones get back to sleeping or whatever."

Meiling ended the call. "I'm wide awake now, but I am still tired, sweetheart. Maybe I will just lay down for a—"

She jumped as her phone, still in her hand, buzzed and rang its annoying tune. "Hello."

"Meiling, this is Wendell."

The president sounded informal again. Did that mean this was more bad news?

"Is everything going okay with the State Department's delivery of mAbs?"

"Yes. But that's not why I am calling."

So it ***was*** more bad news.

"Thank you for your quick response with the Air Guard. They saved our two production facilities."

"Yes, they did. I'm calling about the FBI agent who survived the attack on your lab."

How did the president even hear about that?

"We just heard that the FBI wants custody of him."

"Yes. But I'm afraid that writ of *habeas corpus* is a death sentence for him," the president said. "I wanted to let your people know that I am trying to protect this man because he can probably identify the instigators of the plot to destroy your team and your work. If the FBI gets custody, I don't think he will survive to incriminate anyone. So, my Attorney General has demanded that the lawyer who issued the writ revoke it immediately or face severe consequences. He'll comply. These leftist lawyers are wimps when their livelihoods and careers are on the line—something they always try to do to us."

"Thank you ... Wendell. I will let our team know."

"One more thing, Meiling. There's a movement afoot by my opponents to start investigating the Marburg Pandemic response in the Senate HELP Committee. That could lead to you and certain members of your team being subpoenaed to testify to the committee. Should that happen, a lawyer will be available to educate you about that process."

"Thank you for letting us know."

"Take care, Meiling. You have some great people at Pierce's lab. I will do my best to watch out for them here in D.C.," President Warrington ended the call.

By the time Meiling dropped her cell on the bed, Ryan was up and dressed.

"So it's Wendell again?" He gave her his mischievous grin.

"The address may have been informal, but the message was anything but."

"Well, what did he have to say?"

"He said the Attorney General will prevent the custody grab by the FBI for the agent injured in the attack on us. I guess that's a good thing. But the other bit of news is rather disturbing."

Ryan took one look at her face and wrapped her up in a warm hug. "It can't be that bad. What did he say?"

"The Senate HELP Committee is going to investigate the President's Marburg response, and we may be subpoenaed to testify."

Ryan's grin was gone. "Sounds like a perjury trap to me."

***

10:00 a.m. Eastern Time, Phisher Headquarters

Abe Borland stepped inside his private study, locked the door, and set up a secure conference call with Marsh McDowell and General Kuo.

The heat was rising gradually in the water where the three found themselves. Kuo's assassin had killed Harold Stein. But the FBI agent in the local police's custody in Colorado was worrisome. Abe must find a way to turn off the burner before the water started to boil.

He got the two men on the line and brought them into the conference call.

"This is General Kuo."

"Marsh here also."

"Have either of you heard what happened with the FBI agent on the loose in Colorado?" Abe paused.

"On the loose? I hope you mean that in a metaphorical sense," Marsh said.

"If he's not in good hands, he's on the loose as far as I'm concerned," Abe said.

"I did hear a rumor that the FBI put some lawyers to work to get custody of that guy," Marsh said. "They sent a writ of *habeas corpus* to the Superior Police, but other rumors say that the Attorney General will stop the request."

Abe blew out a blast of frustration. "If the local police have him, he's still a loose cannon waiting to go off at any moment."

"It's okay, Abe. The man can only ***go off*** on Stein. But Stein's dead, and there's no way to connect him to us."

"Maybe," Abe said. "On another note, the Senate HELP Committee is rattling sabers like they want to investigate the president for how he conducted his Marburg response."

"There you go," Marsh said. "We wanted a way to shut down Dr. Chen-Adams's Marburg work. The military approach has failed. We're 0 for 2. But this might allow us to implement the legal approach we were looking for. All we need to do is ask a question that paints the good doctor in a bad light and get her to lie to Congress or say something that we can interpret as a lie. She and possibly some of her cohorts would be convicted of felonies. If we can do that, she's out of a job and perhaps in jail."

"True, Marsh. But does that guarantee that Phisher or Mercer Medical can take over management of the pandemic response? After all, the good doctor's therapeutics are working worldwide."

"But we have mRNA vaccines nearly ready to go," Marsh said.

"***Nearly*** being the operative word. We could ask for an EUA."

General Kuo spoke for the first time. "I do not understand all the legal technicalities you have mentioned, but I—as you Americans say—get the drift. But please remind me what an EUA is."

"General, it's an Emergency Use Authorization."

"Oh, yes. Like for COVID. Nobody can sue."

"That's right," Abe said. "It indemnifies us. We are not held liable."

"Let's set that idea aside for the moment." Marsh paused. "What if we could show that the mAbs and the killer protein being distributed are dangerous?"

"But the whole world is comfortable with using her therapeutics. They are holding the pandemic in check."

"That could change instantly based upon one cleverly planned presentation," Marsh said. "I would need to testify at that hearing and to present stats clearly showing that the mAbs created by Meiling Chen-Adams is failing and causing many deaths. As CDC Chief Operating Officer, I have the credentials to present the data, but I need some bright minds to cherry-pick the data for me to make our case."

Abe chuckled. "My testing team members at Phisher are the cherry-picking champs of the industry. We'll get the data for you. You present it convincingly, Marsh, and we will be in business again. We'll be in the driver's seat."

"If you have difficulty analyzing the data, I can provide some excellent mathematicians," General Kuo said.

"We'll keep that in mind," Abe said. "We have a plan, but we need to hurry. We must be ready to present our data when the committee starts hearing testimony."

"There is another person, a mathematician who might appear less biased than me," Marsh said. "He works for Senator O'Hare."

Chapter 22

Early the next morning, the Senate HELP Committee meeting room in the Senate Dirksen Office Building

Eight o'clock in the morning in D.C. was six o'clock to Meiling. She had gotten up at 3:30 a.m. to fly with the team to the Senate HELP Committee hearing.

President Warrington had provided a lawyer who spent fifteen minutes briefing Meiling on procedures for the hearing and a few details on American law and the Constitution.

At precisely 8:00 a.m., the chairwoman, Senator Sharon Moore from Florida, briefed them on the order of events, the time limits for senators to question the witnesses and the permission that had been granted to question Meiling for a member of Senator O'Hare's staff. Ross Putnam, a man with a Ph.D. in Mathematics from MIT, would do the questioning. Putnam would be the last to ask questions in order to comply with Senate rules regarding staff-member participation.

The chairwoman reminded everyone that the senators questioning Meiling would go in order of seniority.

Meiling and all her team members had submitted written testimony. But when the witnesses were called to be sworn in today, only Meiling was called.

So it was all to be on her shoulders. Maybe their enemies in the Senate thought this might cause her to make mistakes, or perhaps she was their target to eliminate from the Marburg response by incriminating her.

Regardless, she would not let them intimidate her. Meiling vowed to glare at them and dare them to try.

Chairwoman Moore opened the testimony time with a rap of her gavel. “We’ve all read the written statements from each member of the Chen-Adams team. So, let’s go straight to the questioning by committee members. We will start with the gentleman from New York, Mr. Halloway.”

Though Halloway wore an expensive suit, the thinning gray hair hanging shaggy over his collar and his bulbous red nose gave him a seedy look. His leering eyes added to Meiling’s impression of the elderly man.

What did Americans call people like him? A dirty old man. That was Meiling’s initial impression.

Senator Halloway looked across the large room to the single row of desks for the witnesses, each equipped with a microphone. He was surveying her as best he could from several yards away and wasn’t leaving anything out.

The evil within this nation that Ryan and Meiling had agreed to oppose was staring at her. Ungodly stares from an ungodly man leading his nation’s government down an ungodly path. It all pointed in one direction … straight to Satan.

Meiling must not forget that this man represented her spiritual enemy because he had already chosen sides and had not chosen well.

She shivered and tried to shake off the chill that Halloway had caused.

“Dr. Chen-Adams, when did you contact the president about managing the Marburg Pandemic?” His wizened voice betrayed years of smoking resulting in damaged lungs.

She needed to set the record straight right from the start and let them know she would not be pushed around by bullies.

“First, I didn’t contact President Warrington. He sought me out and contacted me. Second, there was no pandemic at that time, only a fear that the CCP would release a Novel Marburg Virus, and if so, the fatality rate would be so high that we could not afford to let it catch us unprepared."

"May I remind you that no reputable authority believes the Chinese released this virus? How do you know that with so much certainty?"

"Sir, may I remind you that you are not a reputable authority to make that statement."

"How dare—"

"Furthermore, I am certain because I treated the first person the CCP infected with this virus."

Halloway's eyes bugged out in a dramatic look of feigned surprise. "You treated patient zero? Whom might that be, pray tell?" He ended with an exaggerated smirk.

"It was Dr. Ling Li, Chief Principal Investigator at the Wuhan BSL-4 Laboratory. He told me how the CCP infected him as punishment both for some indiscretion and to force him to carry this deadly virus to the United States."

Murmuring of many voices spread throughout the room.

The gavel smacked on the sounding block. "May I please have order?"

The room quieted quickly.

"You may continue."

Halloway rubbed his chin for a few seconds. "What motivated this Dr. Li, Chief Principal Investigator at the Wuhan Lab, to seek ***you***?"

"He knew of my work with the class of RNA viruses, of which Marburg is one of the deadliest members. He believed that no one else could save his life."

"No one else in this ***whole*** world? Only ***you*** could save Dr. Li's life?"

"That is correct, Senator Halloway. Only God, or me, or both. Dr. Li didn't believe in God at the time, so he chose me."

"And you don't think highly of yourself, do you?"

Heat rose until it burned her neck and cheeks. Meiling glared at Senator Halloway. "You pompous, condescending, little—"

"Meiling, don't!" Ryan's voice.

The murmuring from the visitors' area behind Meiling rose to a low rumble.

Senator Moore's gavel smacked twice on the block. "Order! Order! I will have order in this room, or I'll have everyone but the committee and the witness removed!"

The room quieted quickly.

Halloway drew a wheezy breath. "Next, Dr. Chen—"

"There will be no next for you, Mr. Halloway. Your time is up."

"Senator Williams from Illinois, you may question the witness."

Senator Alice Williams was a short, rotund lady well past sixty. Her dyed hair seemed more blonde than gray, which did not match her age.

"Dr. Chen, how did the funding of your work by the federal government come about?"

"I am married now. It's Chen-Adams." She paused, but the senator didn't reply. "The president feared the CCP was planning to start another pandemic."

"Another pandemic?" The senator rolled her eyes and muttered something that sounded like whatever.

Meiling chose to ignore the senator's attempted disparagement.

"Yes. Another pandemic. Far worse than COVID-19. And I had the information to substantiate his fears. I understood the CCP because I spent nearly two years working with them. And I had made a breakthrough in virology that could thwart the plans being made by the CCP and PLA." She paused.

The senator remained silent, so Meiling continued.

"The president called Ryan and me and arranged a face-to-face meeting with our team. We met at Camp David, and he told us about the threats from the CCP and how he did not have a good means to combat the medical threats from diseases, biowarfare."

"What was your response to the president's perceived needs?"

"We had our entire core team at the Camp David meeting, so we estimated what it would take to counter the threats from the CCP."

"You asked him for money?"

"No. We told him the level of effort it would take, and he asked us to estimate the cost of maintaining that effort to thwart the biowarfare threat. So, we estimated the ongoing costs, and he said he would fund them."

"He offered to fund your work all on his own?"

"He had our liaison officer with him. But, yes, Senator Williams. All on his own. After all, he does have emergency powers to make those kinds of decisions and to fund the efforts to maintain national security."

"And you know this after being in the U.S. for about four or five months?"

"Closer to six months."

"Long enough to latch onto a man, get married, thus gaining citizenship. And if I'm not mistaken, you are pregnant."

"And you, ma'am, are crude, crass, and a pathetic old—"

Meiling's body jerked at the sharp sound of the gavel striking the block on the chairwoman's desk. "That's enough from both of you. This will be an orderly and mannerly discussion, won't it, Senator Williams?" The chairwoman glared at the rude senator.

Senator Williams nodded.

"Then continue, Dr. Chen-Adams."

"I was trying to tell you that I was raised in Hong Kong partly before the handover from the UK to the People's Republic of China in 1997. We valued our freedom and studied its greatest exponent, the American Constitution. I also know about the Public Health Service Act of 1994—"

"***You***, a young woman fresh from China, are schooling ***me***, a U.S. senator for thirty years, on constitutional law and the president's powers?"

"Thirty years. Does that mean you know what's in the Public Health Service Act, enacted in 1994?"

The chairwoman tapped her gavel lightly to get Meiling's attention.

She looked up at Senator Moore.

"Dr. Chen-Adams, please confine yourself to answering the questions rather than asking them."

"Senator Moore, if Senator Williams insists on revealing her ignorance of the subject, am I not allowed to remove that ignorance so we can get to the truth?"

"Madam Chairman, I object to—"

"This is not a court of law, Senator Williams. I chair this committee, not you." She paused. "If you both can keep this civil, I am inclined to hear what Dr. Chen-Adams has to say." She nodded toward Meiling.

"The act passed in 1994 said that in a national emergency, the president could use his or her discretion to address public health emergencies. The president could enter into contracts to investigate causes and develop treatments for and preventions of diseases. The president's authority comes from the principle of necessity, just like for a military commander. And the president can use available resources to alleviate the people's suffering without having to get permission from the … uh, bureaucrats."

Someone in the back of the audience began clapping. The clapping spread until Senator Moore smacked her gavel again.

"Your time's up, Senator Williams, the chairwoman said. "Let me sum up what you said, Dr. Chen-Adams. The president contracted with your team to thwart the CCP and PLA biowarfare program based on the authority given to him in the Constitution and U.S. Code."

"Thank you, Senator Moore. That is what I tried to communicate."

"The gentleman from Vermont may now question the witness."

Senator Robert Ness adjusted his mic. "Ms. Chen-Adams ..."

"Yes, Robert?"

Several chuckles sounded from behind Meiling.

The senator cleared his throat. "***Dr.*** Chen-Adams, are you familiar with the FBI agent being detained under the custody of the Superior Police Department in Colorado?"

"No, senator. I'm only familiar with one man, my husband. So, I'm not familiar with that man. Are you?"

The hearing room echoed a loud burst of laughter.

Senator Ness's bushy eyebrows pinched until they touched. "Let me rephrase that question, doctor. Are you aware that an FBI agent is being detained by the Superior Police Department?"

"Yes. He was among the twenty FBI agents who tried to kill my team and me and to destroy Dr. Pierce's lab where we do our work."

"I only asked if you knew he was in custody."

"And I verified that I was aware and told you how I became aware."

"Are you saying that you did not receive a call from the president and have a discussion about this FBI agent?"

"No, I am not saying that. How did you become aware of the president's private call to me? By way of a FISA warrant?"

Murmuring throughout the conference room grew from a buzz to a rumble after Meiling's question implying a serious felony on the part of Senator Ness.

"Please stick to answering the questions asked of you, Dr. Chen-Adams." The chairwoman gave Meiling a sharp, reprimanding glance.

Meiling nodded.

"Did the president call you about this matter?"

"Yes, he did."

"And why pray tell, would he do that?"

"Perhaps because this man tried to kill me and was an FBI agent. Doesn't that strike you as strange?"

"And did the president mention a writ of *habeas corpus* requesting the prisoner be transferred to FBI custody?"

"Yes. And doesn't that sound strange to you? As we Americans say, the fox being let into the hen house—the FBI taking custody of their own agent who, disguised as a member of the terrorist organization GTI, tried to kill my co-workers and me."

"Just answer my question, please."

"I did, sir. I said yes."

"And did the president say what he intended to do about the writ?"

"No."

"Tell me the truth, Dr. Chen-Adams."

"Are you calling me a liar, senator?"

"I'm asking you to tell me the truth."

"I swore to tell the truth, and that's precisely what I am doing. No, the president did not say anything about him taking action regarding the writ of *habeas corpus.*"

"But I have evidence that—"

"You had better not have evidence to the contrary, or either you, or your information source, or both are guilty of a serious crime."

"Let me rephrase the question. Did the president say he was going to stop the writ?"

"No, he did not. He said the Attorney General requested that the writ be revoked."

"And the president had nothing to do with the Attorney General's decision?"

"He told me nothing in that regard. If you think otherwise, senator, you are badly mistaken, just like the informant who gave you your bad '*evidence to the contrary*'."

The gavel sounded again. "Dr. Chen-Adams, please eliminate your commentary. Simply answer the questions."

"Even if the answer is misleading and hides the truth rather than reveals it?"

"Whether it's true or not is for the committee to decide, doctor," the chairwoman said.

"Senator Moore, the truth is true no matter what this committee decides."

"That's enough, doctor. Do not speak again in this hearing unless it is to answer a question directly, or I will hold you in contempt."

"Some people in this room I already hold in contempt."

The gavel slammed on the block with a startling noise.

"This hearing is recessed for fifteen minutes. Sergeant at Arms, please escort Meiling Chen-Adams to my office."

Meiling did not expect to be goaded and accused of lying while giving testimony. Maybe she had gotten a bit out of line, but nobody, especially an old reprobate senator, was going to bully her.

The sergeant at arms, a rather large man, hooked Meiling's elbow and escorted her out of the conference room and down the hallway. The chairwoman followed a short distance behind.

Being pulled along by the sergeant at arms, Meiling felt like a school kid being taken to the office to be disciplined.

After Meiling and the sergeant at arms entered Senator Moore's office, she stepped in behind them, closed the door, and circled Meiling until they stood face-to-face.

"Look, Meiling. I understand what you are trying to do—not be bullied by people who are, shall I say, less intelligent than you."

"Don't you mean less moral?"

"Even if that is the case, you must act mannerly and respectfully though they do not."

"You mean like Senator Halloway."

"Yes, even if they act like Senator Gus Halloway from New York. If you promise me that you will behave for the rest of the questioning, we will go back to the committee room and complete the questions. If not, I will hold you in contempt, and the rest of your time in D.C. will not be pleasant. So, what will it be?"

"I promise, Senator Moore."

"Good." She paused. "When a scientist of your stature testifies, the committee usually shows more respect. If you didn't look so young, they probably would not try to pick on you."

"I've dealt with that problem ever since I left Hong Kong. And the CCP scientists added sexual harassment to the mix."

"Let's go back to the committee room and finish the questioning. I think you'll like the next senator much more than the last three. And since the leftists have four people taking potshots at you and the conservatives only one, he will get four times seven minutes." Senator Moore gave Meiling a warm smile.

They returned to the HELP Committee's room without the sergeant at arms holding onto Meiling.

When Meiling sat, Ryan covered his mic with his hand. "How did it go?"

"Your mic is not on, Ryan. And it went well."

"So, they aren't calling you an insurrectionist?" He grinned.

"No. But I have a few names I would like to call Senator Halloway."

The gavel sounded, and Meiling straightened in her chair.

"The hearing will continue now. The gentleman from Idaho may now question the witness."

Senator Jedediah Stokes was the youngest to question Meiling so far. He looked about forty, had short hair, and an athletic build, Senator Halloway's antithesis.

He gave Meiling a warm smile. "Dr. Chen-Adams, would you please give us a summary of why you left China and of the things you have experienced leading up to today where you are serving this nation at the president's request."

Meiling told her story and tried to shorten it. But so much had happened in the last six months that when she finished, the clock said she had taken a half hour to tell her story.

"And that is how a virologist from the Hong Kong Medical University came to the United States by way of Wuhan, China, and now serves America at the request of President Warrington."

There was brief clapping from several journalists that sat in the audience, and there was one hearty amen.

"Mr. Ross Putnam, a member of Senator O'Hare's staff, may now question the witness."

The skinny man with horn-rimmed glasses sat at the right end of the row of committee members. "Dr. Chen-Adams, how many countries are there in the world?"

Where was this line of questioning going? "I believe there are one hundred ninety-five independent sovereign nations in the world."

"And how many have you reached with your Marburg therapeutics?"

“In the U.S., it has been almost eight weeks since we began manufacturing mAbs and seven weeks since we began manufacturing the killer protein. Factories in Europe and India have been manufacturing both therapeutics for about three weeks. In that time, we have reached almost one hundred nations, though the population of many countries is only partly reached.”

“A hundred nations … so, you’ve reached a little over half of the planet.”

“Heavens, no. As a mathematician, you know that you cannot simply count countries. You must count the people reached.”

“So, you mean we must count the number of the sick that were reached and treated and the percentage of those who were saved and who died?”

“Yes, that’s one way to look at it.”

“Looking at it that way, in the Central African Republic, there are five and a half million people, and you treated how many sick people, Dr. Chen-Adams?”

“I do not have the exact number at hand.”

“Would it be fair to say it was around two hundred fifty thousand?”

“That sounds about right. The rest of the people were protected by quarantining the sick.”

“How many died after taking your mAbs?”

“Of those we gave the mAbs infusions to before they reached the onset of organ failure, I know of none that died.”

“Not even one?”

“No, Mr. Putnam. Not even one anywhere in the world.”

“How do you explain the nearly two hundred and fifty who died after taking your infusion?”

Now she had an inkling of where this man was headed with his questions. “They were murdered.”

Putnam emitted harsh, derisive laughter. "Murdered? How convenient. Just when your treatment failed, you say they were murdered."

"Senator Moore." Dr. Pierce was on his feet with a hand raised.

"Dr. Pierce, the chair recognizes you. What reason do you have for interrupting the testimony at such a critical juncture?"

"Dr. Chen-Adams is unaware of a critical piece of information related to the question Mr. Putnam asked. May I approach the witness to give her that information?"

"This is not a trial in a court of law, doctor. Yes, you may give her the information."

"I object," Putnam bellowed.

"Mr. Putnam, this is my hearing, and you do not have the privilege of objecting. Dr. Pierce, you may confer with Dr. Chen-Adams."

"This is outrageous. She is going to be given a way of lying her way—"

"One more word like that, Mr. Putnam, and the sergeant at arms will escort ***you*** out of here."

What information could Robert have that Meiling was unaware of? She waited as he made his way to her.

Robert covered her mic with his hand. "I silenced my cell when we entered the building, but I just received a text from Colonel West. He said to tell you that the investigation into the two State Department pilots was at a critical stage and must not be mentioned in this hearing as it may jeopardize the case."

"Great. What ***can*** I say without tainting the investigation?"

"Tell them that we suspect there is an ongoing investigation, and that you cannot tell them more at this time."

"That will not go over well."

"But it's all we can do, Meiling."

"Thanks, Robert."

Pierce uncovered the mic and returned to his seat.

Putnam continued. "Back to the murder of over two hundred Central Africans who took your mAbs infusion—what made these deaths murder and not a failure of your treatment?"

"The mAbs in that shipment were cooked. We verified that. Heating the mAbs renders them completely ineffective. Somebody wanted people in the Central African Republic to die. The investigation into who did it and why is ongoing, and I'm not allowed to reveal any more than that."

"And you expect us to believe you, a doctor with her reputation and her therapeutics in question?"

"Personally, I do not give a rip what you believe, Mr. Putnam. I gave you the truth, and you can—"

"Meiling, don't." Ryan grabbed her hand again.

Once again, the gavel sounded. "I will have order in this room. Finish your questions, Mr. Putnam. You have one minute. And if anyone disrupts the hearing, I will have them thrown out. Now, wrap it up, Mr. Putnam."

"Dr. Chen-Adams, do you still assert that no one has died after taking your mAbs infusion?"

"Correction. I said I knew of no one not already in organ failure who died after taking my mAbs infusion. The same is true of my killer protein."

"I have presented evidence to the contrary, doctor."

"You have presented an opinion based on your ignorance of the facts, Mr. Putnam."

Putnam's face contorted into an ugly caricature of itself, and he opened his mouth to speak.

"Your time is up, Mr. Putnam," the chairwoman said. "That concludes the testimony for this hearing. Witnesses are excused now. Committee members will remain in the room while we evaluate the testimony we have heard today."

Senator Moore banged the gavel, and the hearing ended.

Meiling's team filed out of the hearing room and gathered in the lobby of the Senate Dirksen Office Building.

"Listen up," Baker said. "We have plenty of time to get to Reagan National, fly home in my Gulfstream, have dinner, and sleep in our own beds tonight. Let's see a show of hands for going home now."

It was unanimous.

As they all climbed into a long limo for their ride to Ronald Reagan Washington National Airport, Meiling received a message from Senator Moore.

Meiling, the committee ruled that we should recommend that your team continue to conduct the President's Marburg response but that you should let us know the findings of the investigation into your cooked mAbs—who did it and why. As always, the vote was along party lines.

A second message followed shortly behind the first.

Senator Ness's familiarity with FBI activities and his line of questioning bothered me, Meiling. Please be watchful for some FBI chicanery.

Chapter 23

Two days later, Pierce's lab compound, 4:00 a.m.

An alert warning sounded from Meiling's cell.

Both Meiling and Ryan sat up in bed.

"I'll check it, sweetheart," Meiling said as she slid out of bed and scooped up her phone.

She turned on the lamp, rubbed her eyes, and did a double take on the cell alert.

"What is it, Meiling?"

"Our security monitors detected an FBI SWAT team. They drove part of the way down our driveway in two vans and are now approaching on foot. They're all decked out in their tactical SWAT team gear."

Ryan was already jumping into a pair of jeans. He pulled on a shirt and then strapped on his gun. "This is their *modus operandi* for terrorizing the people they arrest for political reasons. With Stein gone, I wonder who sicked them onto us."

"Ryan ... they're coming to arrest ***me***."

"Last time, they came for all of us."

"This time is different. I am the only one who testified to the Senate committee. They will probably say that I lied to Congress, which is a felony."

A second alert sounded on her cell phone.

"The message says Rafe has been notified and is on his way to the airport."

She pulled jeans and a blouse from a dresser. "I'm not going to be drug out of my home in my pajamas like they've done to other people."

Ryan slipped into his running shoes. “Who said they’re even going to make it through our gate? And Rafe has that bullhorn we ordered installed on the Huey. It’s like the ones the cops used in Minneapolis and Rochester. We may be able to talk to these guys, to reason with them.”

“I do not think so, sweetheart. But we cannot make a practice of killing FBI agents.”

“You sure as heck aren’t going to give yourself up to them, Meiling.”

“But what if that is the only way to keep our people safe?”

“Meiling, Rafe, and the Huey can keep us safe. Baker and Buck are probably outside by now. I’m going too. Stay inside until we get a handle on what’s happening.”

“Then go, Ryan. I’ll wait here and pray.”

“If you hear any shooting, stay away from the north and west walls. I love you, Meiling. See you in a bit.”

Ryan had barely closed the door when her cell rang. An incoming voice call from Colonel West.

“This is Meiling.”

“This is West. Meiling, we just learned that a team of the FBI’s worst scoundrels was dispatched late yesterday to attempt to arrest you. They have been promised big rewards if they can get you. And these guys don’t play by the rules, so don’t surrender to them no matter what they say. If you do, you won’t live through the day. Use whatever means your people have to stop this group. They’ll probably come dressed in SWAT gear and have been known to carry H&K MP5 submachine guns.”

“They are already here, colonel. They are approaching the lab compound, and it will be dark here for another hour. Our men will use their guns to try to hold them off until our Huey Cobra arrives.”

“My advice, Meiling, is that if your people’s lives are in danger, don’t hesitate to take these rogue cops out.”

"Thanks for letting us know. I'll pass the info to Ryan and Baker."

Meiling ended the call and immediately texted Ryan, Baker, Buck, and Robert, conveying what Colonel West had said. And she added a second message.

Should I call the Superior Police?

Ryan replied immediately.

Do not call the police. They will either stop when they see an FBI SWAT team, or they will get their officers killed.

Ryan was right. She had not been thinking clearly.

Was there anything Meiling could do? She couldn't protect all their people, but she could protect up to six of them—Jinghua, Ming, Robert, Lee, and herself. Maybe only five of them.

There were six positive pressure suits ready to go for the BSL-4 lab. Shauna and the twins would have to stay in their apartment, but five people could retreat to the BSL-4 lab. The FBI wouldn't enter and would not be foolish enough to try to blow up the lab and infect everyone, including their men.

The BSL-3 lab had been scrubbed, but maybe putting Shauna and the girls in that lab would deter the FBI should they enter the building.

That left Meiling with the problem of getting all eight of them from their apartments, across the parking area, and to the lab without making them targets for the approaching FBI. Ryan could help with that.

She composed a text message.

What if we hid Jinghua, Ming, Robert, Lee, and me in the BSL-4 lab and put Shauna and the twins in the BSL-3 lab? We could tell the FBI not to disturb either lab, or they would be infected.

The reply came back in a few seconds.

Only as a last resort.

Regardless, we must get them to the lab building before

the shooting starts.

The shooting could start any second because we can't see them, and we're sure they have night vision. And that's another reason we think they will attack before twilight—sometime in the next 30 minutes.

***

20 minutes later

A burst of fire from an automatic rifle sent Ryan sprawling on his face behind a two-foot-high concrete wall separating the shrubbery from the walkway to the lab building.

Bits of concrete stung as they sprayed his jean-covered legs.

Another burst sounded, and bullets screamed their complaint as they caromed off Baker's temporary shelter. The large boulder had been placed in the compound to separate the parking area from the delivery dock.

"Baker, are you okay?"

"Yeah. But it's not light enough to see those guys except for their gun flashes. I'm calling Rafe to see where he is. He should have been here by now."

Baker scurried to the concrete wall and slid onto his rear beside Ryan. The speakerphone was on.

"This is Rafe."

"Baker here. We're outmanned and outgunned. They've got us pinned down. Where are you, bro?"

"I'm sitting by the hangar. The transmission oil pressure gauge is reading zero. The temperature's okay, but I'm not sure what's causing the pressure to read zero. My best guess is that it's a false reading."

"Rafe, if you're guessing wrong, won't it destroy the transmission?"

"Yes. But how long can you guys hold out?"

"About five to ten minutes, depending."

"If I engage the transmission and the temperature reading stays in the normal range, then I can be reasonably sure that the pressure gauge is giving bogus readings."

"Yeah," Baker said. "And without the Huey Cobra, we're into desperate measures here, bro. Things like telling the FBI to back off or we're gonna vent the BSL-4 lab exhaust at them. But we can't do that very well unless you're here with the bullhorn we installed on the Cobra."

"Okay, I'm giving it a try."

Ryan's cell sounded the alarm for an incoming message. "Pierce says he's in the conference room and has the radio on, so he can talk to you when you're airborne. We can relay messages for the FBI through Pierce to you. So be ready when you arrive, Rafe."

"Right now, just trying to get this bird in the air. Here goes."

The wop, wop turned to a syncopated roar.

"Looks good so far. Taking off now. Call Pierce on your cell. He'll hear from me on the radio in a few minutes. If all goes well, I'll be there a couple of minutes after that."

Ryan called Pierce and gave him the timetable for the Huey's arrival. He also told Pierce about Meiling's idea for using the labs to keep the FBI away.

"I thought about that. It might work, depending on the stubbornness of the FBI team leader. But it doesn't protect you two. So let's keep it in our pocket and only pull it out if needed."

"Sounds good," Ryan said. "Baker, why haven't we heard any more shooting? Twilight is almost here."

"Yeah. They're probably creeping closer, but the lights at the gate are a problem for them. They can't approach the gate."

Three short bursts of automatic rifle fire sounded.

The lights at the gate went out.

"The gun flashes are near the leading edge of the rubble that used to be trees," Baker said.

"We could use some more rubble that used to be rogue FBI agents," Ryan said. "I'm calling Pierce to see if he's heard from Rafe on the radio."

Ryan called Pierce's cell. It rang five times and was about to go to voice mail when Pierce answered.

"This is Ryan. Any word from Rafe?"

"He's on his way but watching that oil pressure gauge like a hawk. So far, so good."

"That means he's about two minutes out," Ryan said. "As soon as Baker and I get a bead on the SWAT team, we'll have a message for them to relay to Rafe."

"I'll be waiting. You two take care out there."

"Will do." Ryan ended the call. "Baker, I'm going to call Meiling. If there's even a remote chance that we may need to put our people in the BSL-3 and BSL-4 labs, she needs to contact them and tell them to get ready. Maybe after Rafe hits the FBI hard, the women, kids, and Lee can make a run for the lab building."

Three or four guns blasted the concrete wall for several seconds.

Ryan buried his head in his arms to keep the concrete shrapnel from hitting his face.

"My eyes have adjusted, and there's a little light now," Baker said. "Look, the gate. They're rushing it."

The guns sounded again in three or four long bursts that sent Ryan and Baker hugging the concrete walkway.

"They're covering the group trying to get through the gate. We've gotta drive them away from it. If they get through, they could capture those still in their apartments," Baker said.

"Including the person they really want, Meiling." Ryan raised and half emptied his fifteen-round magazine at the spot he'd seen rifle flashes moments before.

When Ryan stopped shooting, another barrage came from the rifles to cover the SWAT team members running for the gate.

Ryan laid back down on the concrete and called Meiling.

She answered immediately. “Are you okay, sweetheart?”

“I’m fine, and Rafe is on his way. If you’re still contemplating hiding people in the two bio-safety labs, you’d better call and tell them.”

“I already called them. We have group conversation going using text messages. I’ll signal them when we can run to the lab building.”

“Meiling, we could be ready for that in a couple of minutes. After Rafe carpet RGPs them, you should be safe to run.”

“I’ll be waiting for you to give me the go-ahead, sweetheart. Please, take care. It sounds like a war out there.”

“That’s a pretty doggone good description. Stand by for my call.”

They ended the call just as Baker shot a long burst from his M4.

“They dropped back from the gate that time, but I can’t hold them off much longer.”

“Listen, Baker.”

From the southeast, the pulsating roar of the Huey grew steadily louder.

“I’d bet they’re listening for that sound, too,” Baker said. They’ll know what happened to the last bunch of FBI agents that attacked this place.”

“What do you think they’ll do?”

What must have been a half-dozen automatic rifles fired simultaneously.

There were probably men breaking through the gate right now. If they came inside, they could easily get to Lee’s, Jinghua’s, or Meiling’s apartments.

Ryan laid down and army-crawled to the far end of the concrete wall. He peeked around the end of it and saw movement at the gate. He raised his Sig Sauer, aimed, emptied his magazine, and pulled his head and shoulders back behind the wall.

A ferocious volley chewed up the end of the concrete wall where Ryan's head had been two seconds before. But he had driven them away from the gate, temporarily.

Ryan glanced back at Baker.

Baker gave him thumbs up, then Baker raised and fired a long volley at the group of retreating men now visible in the twilight.

The Huey Cobra swooped down, leveled, and fired a two-second burst of RPGs from its M129 grenade launcher at seven grenades per second.

The entire area outside the compound gate disappeared in an explosion of smoke and dust.

Thirty seconds later, the dust had drifted far enough away to see from the gate to the rubble of the former forest.

Ryan saw no movement, so he called Meiling.

She answered immediately.

"Now, Meiling. Get everyone to the lab building."

"I had the text ready. Just sent it. I'm going out the door right now. See you soon, sweetheart."

Though they could see no members of the SWAT team now, Rafe was talking to them through to powerful bullhorn as he hovered to the southeast of the gate, a hundred yards from where the SWAT team had been when he fired.

"Do not, I repeat, do not approach the gate, or I will send a volley of RPGs like you have never seen. In addition, if you pose any further threat to the lab, we will divert the exhaust from the BSL-4 lab toward you. This air will contain Novel Marburg, Nipah virus, Zaire Ebola, Hantavirus, and a few other deadly pathogens currently in the lab. You will not survive as there are no therapeutics for any but the Novel

Marburg Virus. Shall I tell you how Zaire Ebola will kill you? Suffice it to say; you will die a horrid death ending with the liquification of all your organs, including your lungs, which will drown in their own juices, so to speak."

Baker grinned. "Rafe has got a flair for the dramatic. I don't think those guys will be back if they even survived Rafe's RPG volley."

Simultaneously, four apartment doors opened. Lee, Jinghua, and Meiling merged as they ran across the parking area toward the lab building.

Shauna and the two small girls followed behind them at a slower pace.

From the corner of his eye, Ryan saw movement near the trees that lay in what had been the outer edge of the forest. It was a man, and he had a rifle.

Evidently, Buck saw the shooter too. He dropped out the old magazine and slammed in another.

Jinghua and Meiling scurried across the center of the parking area toward the shelter of the lab.

"Get down, now!" Ryan tried to make his voice heard over the whining of the Huey.

The shooter's gun raised toward the two women.

Buck raised his gun.

Jinghua pushed Meiling to the ground, and as she fell on top of Meiling, the crack of the rifle sounded. The crack came an instant before Buck fired.

The shooter went down and stayed down.

Buck knelt beside the women.

Jinghua had landed on Meiling. She had tried to cover Meiling's body with her own.

A large pool of blood formed underneath the two women.

***

Buck looked down in disbelief at the growing pool of blood. Why couldn't he have been faster?

There was more blood now, and he was helpless.

Meiling slid out from under Jinghua and looked from the blood to the hole ripped into the lower part of Jinghua's shoulder.

Tears flooded Meiling's face as she tried to pack the wound with Jinghua's blouse to slow the bleeding.

"What can I do to help?"

"Just a minute." Meiling ripped off the entire sleeve of her long-sleeved blouse and pulled it tightly around Jinghua's slender body.

"Buck, I cannot tie it tight enough. Help me."

"What do you want me to do?"

"Pull it tight. Very tight. Then tie one overhand knot and hold it with your fingers while I finish tying it off."

Blood had continued to pool under Jinghua's shoulder. Too much blood.

Meiling glanced up at Buck's face. Had she read the message in his eyes?

Can anyone live with such blood loss?

Buck's breathing turned to panting as he watched the very lifeblood of this brave young woman draining onto the pavement of the parking lot.

Buck looked at Meiling.

Her face was tightly drawn. "The bullet went through below her shoulder, but this is serious."

"How serious?" He choked on his words.

"I do not know. We know she's bleeding a lot. There are the subclavian artery and vein to worry about and the brachiocephalic artery and vein. If the blood is coming from one of those arteries, she is in serious trouble."

Rafe had landed the Huey outside the gate. He came running through the gate and stopped beside them.

Meiling looked up at Rafe. "You need to get her to a trauma center. The nearest Level 1 trauma center is in Denver, Denver Health. It is one of the best in the world. It's about twenty miles from here."

Buck blew out a blast of worry and frustration. "Then we're going to the best. Rafe, you've got to fly us to Denver Health."

"Buck, the Huey can only seat two pilots."

"I'll take the back seat, lean it back, and put her on top of me." He gently scooped up Jinghua. "Come on, Rafe. We're going now. How long will it take?"

They both started moving toward the Huey, with Meiling following them.

"Once we lift off, we'll land in about three minutes," Rafe said.

"I don't know if she's got three minutes," Meiling said.

"Then let's go, bro. Pedal to the metal," Buck said.

Jinghua's eyelids fluttered and opened. She stared up into his eyes. "Buck, please just hold me, and I'll be okay."

"I'm calling Denver Health now to tell them you're coming," Meiling said. "Look for the big cross, Rafe. I think it's on top of the trauma center building."

Jinghua's eyes closed.

Chapter 24

6:10 a.m. Denver Health, Denver, Colorado

As the Huey touched down on the big white cross on top of the trauma center at Denver Health, Buck studied the people to whom he would be entrusting this young woman for whom he was fast falling.

In the doorway beside the helipad, a trauma stretcher sat surrounded by a team of people in scrubs, each with various instruments in their hands or hanging from them.

As welcome as that sight was, the sick ache in the pit of Buck's stomach threatened to send him to the restroom, where he would lose whatever was left from last night's dinner. But he couldn't let that happen now. He needed to know what they were doing for Jinghua and where they were taking her.

With his shirt blood-soaked from Jinghua laying on top of him for the ride to the hospital, he slid through the rear-seat door of the Huey and handed Jinghua to a tall man who had the bearing of a doctor.

After Buck slid out and his feet hit the ground, a nurse studied his blood-drenched shirt. "Are you hurt too?"

"No. I carried her to this bird and held her all the way here. Do you know if ... if we got her here soon enough?"

"She's young. It appears that you did all the right things. We'll know more after we check vital signs and start the transfusion."

Seconds later, Jinghua was on the trauma stretcher rolling into the trauma center.

Rafe stuck his head out the open front door of the Huey. "Buck, they said I had to move my bird. They may need to use the helipad again in a few minutes. I'll meet you down in emergency."

Buck gave Rafe a thumbs up. It was only an acknowledgment that he'd heard Rafe, not a commentary on Buck's dreadful feelings welling up inside.

Worry that he might lose something he'd never had before kept intruding, colliding with his faith, threatening to derail it. From the first chance Buck had to spend time with Jinghua, he found her to be cute, intelligent, warm, caring, and somehow innocent though she had spent more than twenty-seven years in a Maoist country where she was educated from pre-school up through her Ph.D. and MD degrees.

Dr. Jinghua Ren was unique on planet earth, and Buck was determined to attempt anything to keep—the truth hit Buck with the force of a Babe Ruth home run hit.

He wanted to keep her alive for himself. And that wasn't necessarily a bad thing, but they had just left Dr. Pierce's lab that had been under attack only minutes before, and not all of the FBI attackers had been accounted for.

Buck pulled out his cell to call Baker.

His cell rang.

It was Robert.

Buck answered.

"How is she, Buck?"

"She's alive, and a trauma team has her now. We'll have to wait a while longer to see how she responds to treatment. What's happening at the lab?"

"While you were taking off in the chopper, Ming called the Superior Police Department."

"How did they respond after that gruesome scene we turned over to them a few days ago?"

"They were a big help. The sniper who shot Jinghua and another FBI goon were the only survivors of Rafe's strafing. The police caught the two scampering up Coal Creek near the head of the lab's driveway. They shot and killed one of them and took the sniper into custody."

"Right now, I'd like to shoot and kill that sniper." Buck growled out the words with a raw ferocity he couldn't control.

"That's what Baker said too."

He took a calming breath. "Is everyone else okay at the lab?"

"I think so. We're all together in the conference room trying to wind down while we watch Shauna's twins run laps around the table, oblivious to all the danger we just experienced."

"Be sure to pray for Jinghua."

"We will, Buck." Robert paused. "After my wife died, I never thought I'd find someone like Ming. We're planning to get married soon. From the looks of it, you and Jinghua are headed in the same direction. If so, don't waste any time, son. There's too much uncertainty in this fallen world."

"Yeah." That was all Buck could manage as his voice choked off and his eyes welled.

"Let us know when you have some news about Jinghua."

"Will do," Buck said, and they ended the call.

Now he needed to track down where they had taken Jinghua and find out how to get status updates.

Buck hurried down the flight of stairs to the main floor of the emergency room as Jinghua's words replayed in his mind.

Buck, please just hold me, and I'll be okay.

Chapter 25

10:00 a.m., Abe Borland's office

Abe waited for status on the SWAT team's arrest of Dr. Chen-Adams. They should have completed their entry into the lab and arrested the doctor by 7:00 a.m. at the latest.

For this operation, Abe had found another contact in the FBI who would provide status for the SWAT team breaching the lab. The agent, Rocky Rhodes, was a friend of Agent Kyle Wagner, the man killed in the ProtSyn assault in Rochester.

With the less-than-stellar record the previous attempts had compiled, it had taken a careful negotiation that permitted Agent Rhodes to remain far from the attack. The man was paranoid about being caught.

At ten o'clock, Abe still had nothing to tell Marsh and General Kuo for their planned 10:30 a.m. conference call.

Abe punched in Rhodes's number.

Rhodes answered on the third ring.

"This is Abe. Why haven't you called me?"

"I parked at the edge of the residential development near Coal Creek, where the driveway takes off toward the lab. I watched the assault with my night vision binoculars."

"Why are you stalling, Rhodes? Tell me what you saw.'

"There was a firefight when the SWAT team tried to get through the gate. The people inside the lab compound held the SWAT team off just long enough for an attack helicopter to come in and shoot some kind of explosives. I'm not certain, but I think the chopper killed all but two of the team members."

Abe swore.

"What happened to the other two?"

"The local cops came in and shot one and arrested the other."

So now the Superior Police had two FBI agents who might rat on the conspirators. But FBI agent number one only knew of Stein being involved. Agent number two, captured today, had been contacted by Rhodes, a man Abe had contacted directly. That was getting too close to home.

The captured man needed to be bought off or silenced permanently, or Abe could be in trouble. So could Marshall McDowell. General Kuo could always slink back to China. It might hurt his career, but he wouldn't spend any time in prison. Abe, on the other hand ...

"Rhodes, did the cops see you there?"

"I witnessed the cops' shooting of one and capture of the other FBI agents as they came up the creek. That's when I knew I had to leave the area before I attracted any attention.

"At one point in my getaway, it seemed the cops might be following me, so I tried to get to Denver and hide in the heavy traffic. By then, it was ten o'clock, and I still hadn't had a chance to call you."

"That's okay. You've reported now. I will take it from here." Abe ended the call.

Should Abe trust that this guy would not be caught and questioned? If he was questioned, could Abe trust him to stay quiet? No. This guy needed to be dealt with, just like Stein. That would be an agenda item for the 10:30 a.m. call with Marsh and Kuo.

At precisely 10:30 a.m., Abe launched the conference call. After he added both men to the call, he told them the story of another failed attempt to use the FBI to get Dr. Chen-Adams.

"Why do you keep trying violent methods of removing Chen-Adams?" Marsh asked. "You failed in the Central African Republic and now twice at their laboratory. The best thing you've tried was to damage a mAbs shipment causing the recipients to die. Chen-Adams sniffed that one out, but there are other means of painting her as a failure without killing anyone, Abe."

"You're probably right," Abe said. "But we have a potential problem that needs to be top priority right now."

"We've failed at everything we've tried except for Stein's assassination. I thought top priority would be shutting this effort down."

"Listen for a minute, Marsh," Abe said. "Agent Rocky Rhodes, the man I used for surveillance today, was a friend of Agent Kyle Wagner, one of the men killed in Rochester. A member of the SWAT team was captured today by the Superior Police. This SWAT team member had contacted Rhodes to coordinate surveillance of today's operation. So there is the potential for the police to link Rhodes to me. And though we have only had a couple of face-to-face meetings, depending on how deep the cops go in their investigation, they could find out that we've been cooperating all along."

"If Rhodes is the link, you're going to propose giving the police a missing link, right, Abe?" Marsh said.

"I don't think we have a choice."

"I have many choices," General Kuo said. "But I cannot cause my country to lose face by claiming diplomatic immunity if the police try to arrest me. So, I should return to China."

Maybe that was best. Kuo had been useful but mostly for the military-type operations and the assassination. There might not be any more of that. Abe could make do without him.

"Yes, general. That might be best for you and your country."

"But as for me ..." Marsh said, "... I could try to deny cooperation with Phisher Pharmaceuticals, but I don't think you would let me do that, would you, Abe?"

"We don't have to let it come to that, Marsh. Besides, you are an accessory to murder, attempted murder, and conspiracy to commit other crimes. No. You need to cooperate with me. We can blame the FBI and government bureaucrats, claim innocence, eventually shut down Dr. Chen-Adams and company, and then take over their role for this pandemic."

"Abe, I ***am*** a government bureaucrat. So where does that leave me in your plan? Before you answer that, you must realize that what you just proposed is the best possible scenario of several. Abe, the best of several possible outcomes is seldom realized."

Marsh was teetering on the edge of bailing out in some way. However he did it, Abe would be left holding the bag when the cops came to arrest the perpetrators.

That thought raised a question. How likely was it that a man like Marsh McDowell would commit suicide? But if he was involved in the attempt to remove Dr. Chen-Adams from her current role and was caught, Marsh might be a suicide candidate. Yes, he would be.

Abe tried to calm his voice so the excitement at using a dead Marshall McDowell to free Abe from all suspicion would not register with Marsh.

Abe's conclusion from this conversation ...

It isn't wise to have a serious conversation with a person while you are contemplating how to kill them. You might give yourself away.

Chapter 26

10:30 a.m. Denver Health trauma center

Buck realized as he stood near the nurses' station in the trauma center that he was holding his arms away from his body so they wouldn't touch the cold, sticky shirt he wore. The shirt probably had a cup or more of Jinghua's blood.

A nurse approached him with a hospital gown in her hand. "Sir, you must put your shirt in that red biohazard bin." She pointed to the large container nearby along the wall. "Here's a hospital gown top you can slip into. It's against policy to run around here half-dressed.

"Nurse, the guy they just escorted down the hallway was only half in his gown. His rear end was—"

"That's an entirely different issue. Now dispose of that shirt. No telling what nasty pathogens are in that blood."

Buck started to tell the nurse who Jinghua was and where she worked, but saying she worked in a BSL-4 lab would not have eased the nurse's mind about the state of his bloody shirt.

He took off the shirt and dropped it into the bin.

She handed him the gown top, and he slipped it on. "Where is the hospital gift store?"

The nurse pointed to the hallway on their left. "It's a bit of a walk to Pavilion B where the gift shop is located. Bet you're looking for a shirt."

Buck nodded and headed down the hallway to replace the gown with any shirt he could find.

In the gift shop, he found an extra-large Denver Broncos t-shirt, bought it, and slipped into it.

Before he made it back to the trauma center, Buck had been stopped by three people asking him what he thought about the Bronco's new quarterback.

When he reached the trauma center lobby, he scurried across it to intercept a man in scrubs emerging from the hallway that led deep into the bowels of the hospital. In those restricted places where Jinghua was being treated, both terrible and wonderful things took place.

By the time Buck reached the scrub-clad doctor, he had stopped and begun a conversation with a young couple about their child.

Wrong doctor.

Buck looked at the wall clock. 10:30 a.m. Three and a half hours had passed since the trauma team took Jinghua away on a trauma stretcher.

He had already bugged the nurse at the emergency room counter more times than he could count trying to get any status on Jinghua.

During that span of time, Rafe had taken the Huey back to a landing spot beside the lab compound.

Baker had called asking about Jinghua and saying he wanted to drive Ming and Meiling to Denver Health, but they were still working with the local police to provide details about the FBI SWAT team that no one wanted to claim.

The Superior Police Department had called FBI Headquarters in D.C., and they had denied any knowledge of an FBI SWAT team operating in Colorado.

Something was definitely fishy, but until he heard the words that told him Jinghua was going to be okay, Buck didn't have the mental capacity to work on that puzzle.

A balding, sixty-something man in scrubs sauntered from the hallway where they had taken Jinghua. He headed toward the nurses' station, and Buck followed him.

When he heard the words "Dr. Jinghua Ren," Buck butted in. "I brought Jinghua here. How is she doing?"

The doctor studied Buck for a few seconds. "If you brought her here in that attack helicopter, you must have changed shirts."

Buck had already heard enough to know that Jinghua must have talked to this man. That must mean good news.

"Dr. Ren is a small woman who lost a large amount of blood. It was touch and go for a bit because she was on the verge of hypovolemic shock, but thanks to you getting her here in just minutes, she should be fine after she regains her strength."

Buck blew out the breath he had been holding. "When can I see her?"

"We'll hold her here overnight, and if she's doing well, she can probably go home tomorrow."

Maybe the doctor didn't hear him. "That's fine, but when can I see her?"

"You know, she's been asking the same question about you. You're a lucky man, Mr. uh—"

"Buck McKinney. And thanks, doctor. I don't know what I'd have done if I'd lost her after just finding her. She works with our team at Dr. Pierce's lab near Superior."

"That's what she told me. That's quite a team you have. Your work has cured the handful of Marburg cases that have come our way. We will keep her here in one of our rooms until she leaves tomorrow."

"You didn't say when I can see her."

"Uh, yes. Our pandemic policies say you can't go into our trauma rooms."

"Doctor, I came in here with a pint of her blood soaked into my clothes. If anyone has the right to see—"

"Let me see what I can do. But I'd suggest you wear that gown top and cover up the Broncos shirt. You need to look like a patient." The doctor rubbed his chin for a moment. "Maybe we can admit you to ensure you weren't infected by all that blood. Yes. That'll work."

Buck shoved his arms through the openings in the shirt, wrapped it around his upper body, and followed the doctor down a hallway lined with emergency care rooms.

The doctor stopped in the doorway of a room. "This is Dr. Harris. I'm coming in, Dr. Ren, and I've brought another patient to see you."

Dr. Harris drew the curtain partially open.

Buck stepped through the opening.

Jinghua's eyes were open, and they widened as recognition lit her face. "Buck, you saved my life." She reached for him with her right arm.

A bandage showed near the top of Jinghua's left shoulder, and she made no effort to move that arm.

Buck moved to her bedside.

Jinghua pulled him down until she hooked his neck. She pulled him closer until she kissed him. "Oh, I shouldn't have done that. My mouth tastes like a chemical factory."

"It's okay. Chemistry was always my favorite subject."

"Buck, was Meiling hurt?"

"No. But I've got to call Meiling in a few minutes to let her know that you're okay. She's probably still bawling her eyes out because you sacrificed yourself."

"Bawling her eyes out? Do you mean crying?"

"Yeah."

"Let me get this straight." Dr. Harris's voice from behind Buck. "Dr. Ren, you took a bullet for Meiling?"

"She pushed Meiling to the ground and laid on top of her," Buck said.

"Is this Meiling, Dr. Meiling Chen-Adams?" Dr. Harris's eyebrows rose.

"That's her. The woman who has saved us from the dirtiest trick China has tried to pull on America and the world."

"So, we have a real heroine right here in the Ernest E. Moore Shock Trauma Center. A doctor who risked her life to save the life of the doctor who's saving America and perhaps the world."

"That about sums it up." Buck grinned and moved his focus from Dr. Harris back to Jinghua.

Jinghua took several deep breaths and closed her eyes.

"Mr. McKinney, we need to let her rest now. You can hide out in the room next door. If anyone bothers you, tell them you're my patient and that I'm checking you out for exposure to contaminated blood."

Jinghua's eyes popped open. "But my blood is not contaminated."

The doctor chuckled. "It was contaminated after it soaked through Buck's shirt." He waved Buck out the door. "Make your phone calls in there. Give her an hour or two of rest before you test the chemical factory. And no explosions, please, or you'll be bounced out of here, son."

Jinghua raised her head. "Dr. Harris, what if I feel better sooner than an hour?"

"You will think you feel fine until you suddenly hit a brick wall, and your energy is all used up. We don't want you going there, young lady." He finished his admonition with an authoritative, pursed lips expression.

"I'll make sure she minds, doc," Buck said as he left the room.

He quickly placed a call to Meiling.

"Buck, how is she doing?"

"I just talked with her, Meiling, and you're not gonna believe this."

"Is it good or bad?"

"It's incredible. She kissed me."

"That ***is*** good news. What did the doctor say?"

"He said not to let the chemi—uh, he said they're going to keep her overnight here at the trauma center and then let her go home tomorrow if she keeps progressing as she has been."

"Rafe flew the Huey up here to the lab. What do you plan to do?"

"I'm gonna stay here until they discharge her tomorrow."

"It's only twelve o'clock. Maybe Ming and I should drive down to Denver and visit with Jinghua too."

"It's against trauma center rules under pandemic policies. They won't let you back here to the trauma care rooms."

"Buck, how did you get in to see her?"

"The doctor made me his patient until tomorrow. So I'm spending the night here."

Meiling giggled. It was a good sign.

"So you are spending the night, huh? Be careful not to let the chemistry get out of hand."

"That's just what the doctor said."

"I'll let everyone know she is doing well. But, Buck, some things have happened while we talked to the police."

"Oh. What happened? The threat of another attack?"

"No. Not exactly. But the Superior Police have questioned two rogue FBI agents, and they both said they were taking orders from FBI Deputy Director Harold Stein, who was recently murdered. And both agents believe Stein was in cahoots with the CEOs of the biggest pharmaceutical companies, all wanting to replace our team as the managers of the president's Marburg response."

"So there still could be some trouble ahead?"

"Yes. But now we know whom to watch," Meiling said.

"That being the case, I think we need to have a chat with Colonel West and President Warrington."

"That's what everyone here is saying," Meiling said. "We cannot depend on the FBI. We've been fortunate so far in that our own defenses have protected us."

"But now the politics could get nasty."

"You take care, Buck, and we will see you tomorrow. Let us know when Jinghua will be discharged."

They ended the call.

This might have been a long night spent in an emergency care room with none of the niceties of a hotel room. But after Buck said good night to Jinghua, he had a problem big enough to chew on all night.

How can management of the Marburg response be stolen from us, and who is capable of doing that?

Chapter 27

The next day, 6:30 a.m. Mountain Time, Denver Health Trauma Center

The pulsating roar of the helicopter was partially muted by Jinghua's lightheadedness. The noise faded as she slowly emerged from the dream planted in her mind by the events of yesterday morning.

Though death had come near, she had not feared it, for Buck's arms held her firmly but gently, and they were both held even more firmly in the arms of the one who would never let them go, Jesus.

Then surprising herself, Jinghua had kissed Buck. And that bold move was not merely an expression of gratitude for saving her life. It expressed her joy at looking forward to the life she might have with this big, cowboy-like pilot, provided he felt toward her as she did toward him.

Her door opened, and the curtain hiding her bed slid back.

"Good morning." The cheerful face of a middle-aged nurse appeared. "It's time to unhook you and let you get cleaned up and ready to go home, provided the doctor hasn't changed his mind."

"My clothes were all saturated in blood. I have nothing to wear home."

"Don't worry. If the folks coming to pick you up can't bring some of your clothes to wear, we can give you something from our clothes closet. The clothes are all new. We have all sizes, but not necessarily the latest styles."

Thirty minutes later, Jinghua lay on her hospital bed again, but now clean, with teeth and hair brushed, and dressed in a fresh hospital gown. The activity had left her fatigued, famished, and thirsty.

She drank half the glass of water by her bed. Then looked up at the nurse.

"We don't usually keep patients here long enough to feed them, but food for you and Mr. McKinney is on its way from the main hospital. I am going to get it right now."

"Thank you." She paused. "Is Buck still asleep?"

"Couldn't sleep much last night."

Jinghua looked up at the tall man in a bright orange Broncos t-shirt and jeans marred by a few blood stains.

The nurse left, and Buck sat in the chair beside her bed.

"I was exhausted. I slept. Why couldn't you sleep?"

"Had too much on my mind."

"If I may ask, what did—"

"You, Jinghua. I thought we might lose you yesterday after the bullet clipped a large artery."

"But you didn't."

"No, I didn't. So, what am I going to do with you?"

"Everything." She blurted out her reply before thinking how Buck might misunderstand it.

"Why don't we start by courting?"

"You are taking me to court?"

He shook his head.

"Is that American for dating?"

"It's more like dating with a purpose. We spend a lot of time together to learn if God is leading us to marry."

"I see. And how long does this dating go on?"

"Until we get our and His answers."

"How long does that take—I mean, usually?"

"For some people, almost no time at all," Buck said, then grinned.

"Buck, I think we are '***some people***'."

Before he could reply, the nurse arrived with their breakfast on a cart.

Buck stood when she entered the room.

The nurse started to set the food on Jinghua's bedside tray.

"I can do that," Buck said.

"Thank you. When you finish breakfast, the doctor should be here to see if we can send you home." She beamed a big smile. "Enjoy, you two."

As soon as the nurse cleared the doorway, Jinghua slid to the side of the bed, swung her feet around, and sat up. She had to wait a few seconds for dizziness to fade.

Buck sat again and slid his chair closer to the bed.

After she noticed Buck admiring the pair of legs she dangled beside the food cart, Jinghua cleared her throat.

That got Buck's attention, and he quickly refocused on the food. "We should eat before the doctor gets here."

"Yes. I am starving. But first, I have something to say."

Buck's blue eyes met her gaze. "What's that?"

"My mouth is no longer a chemical factory."

"Mine neither." Buck slid his chair even closer. He leaned toward her until their foreheads touched. "You are so beautiful, even after spending a night in a trauma center."

"Beautiful? Buck, you cannot even see me. We are too close."

"Not too close for this." He kissed her, and there were no chemical contributions to shorten it, only some cogent chemistry to keep it going long enough for Jinghua to realize what she had found in America.

Buck leaned back in his chair, and their gazes locked for several seconds.

"Buck, who will be first, Robert and Ming or us?"

"Why not a double wedding?"

"That would be good, provided they do not, as we Americans say, dillydally."

Chapter 28

The next day, 9:00 a.m. Mountain Time, Meiling's apartment

Meiling looked across their dining table and studied Ryan for a moment.

He looked calm as he sipped the last of his morning coffee.

"Why do you suppose the president wants us all to attend a video meeting with him this morning? He wouldn't even tell us why we all needed to be there. And Kendall Conroe called us twice to verify that we would all be there."

"We'll find out in about an hour. Don't worry about it. If there were any danger to us, he would have warned us. This must be something else—a policy change, changes to our orders, something like that."

At 09:55 a.m. Meiling and Ryan walked into the conference room where Robert and Ming were lining up chairs in two rows along one side of the table, and a single laptop sat on the table in front of the chairs.

Buck and Jinghua, with one arm in a sling, sat at one end of the two rows of chairs, and they were visible on the big flatscreen monitor on the opposite wall.

"It looks like we're going to be on TV." Ryan pointed at the images of Buck and Jinghua on the monitor.

"I think President Warrington just wants to see all of us while he talks to us," Meiling said.

The door opened, and the rest of the group filed in, including Shauna and the twins, Deborah and Sarah.

"Yes, he does want to see all of us, and he wants all of us to be seen," Dr. Pierce said. So, short people in the front row and taller ones in the back. Shauna, you and the twins can take the end seats in the front row in case you need to take the girls out. Jinghua, you, Meiling, and Ming complete the front row, and the rest of us will sit in the back row."

"What's this all about, Robert?" Baker said.

"I wasn't told any details except to arrange for everyone to be seen by the president. He has some announcement to make. We'll have to wait—no, we won't have to wait, we're going live now with President Warrington and a national TV audience."

"National audience? This oughta be interesting, y'all," Buck said.

President Warrington appeared on the flatscreen monitor. "Good morning, gentlemen, Baker, Buck, Ryan, Robert, and Lee. Good morning, ladies, Shauna and her twins and Jinghua, Meiling, and Ming.

"I have asked you to come this morning because I, the rest of the American government, and the American people want to thank you for your heroic service during the Marburg Pandemic. If it weren't for you and your efforts, this biologically engineered disease would have caused devastating loss of life throughout the United States and every other nation across the globe. The magnitude of the depopulation from a ninety percent mortality rate would have set civilization back a hundred years or more.

"Therefore, for Dr. Meiling Chen-Adams teams' persistence against incredible odds and for winning the battle against the Novel Marburg Virus through their skill and ingenuity, I am awarding each of you here today the Presidential Medal of Freedom. Well, the twins, Deborah and Sarah, will have to wait their turn for such an award, maybe in twenty-five years or so.

"The team completed their historic work while facing vicious attempts at character assassination, continuous danger, and savage armed attacks from the CCP and malefactors within the U.S., including rogue federal government members.

"And based on events from two days ago, one of these medals will be given ***with distinction*** to Dr. Jinghua Ren for sacrificing her life for Dr. Meiling Chen-Adams by covering Meiling with Jinghua's own body and taking a bullet meant for Meiling. It took the heroic efforts of Meiling, pilots Rafer Jackson and Buck McKinney, and an excellent trauma team at Denver Health trauma center to save Jinghua's life. We are so thankful she is with us today.

"Because of national security concerns, I cannot provide you with many of the incredible accomplishments of this team. Suffice it to say that they have done the impossible in multiple situations.

"Now for the presentation of the medals ..."

President Warrington had flown his chief of staff, Kendall Conroe, and the team's liaison, Colonel Obadiah West, to present the medals. They handed them out, one by one, as the control camera on the president's end zoomed in on each recipient.

After the presentations, President Warrington gave some closing remarks and told the team that they were off the air.

"Please remain in the conference room for a few minutes. We have some information that is for your ears only."

***

10:30 a.m. Eastern Daylight Time, Abe Borland's office

Abe had sat alone in his office for an hour and a half and hadn't heard anything official. However, Marsh McDowell should have committed suicide by now ... with a little help from a professional assassin.

If one is seeking world prominence, sometimes it's necessary to kill a friend, especially if it keeps one out of prison and keeps one's dreams alive.

But that still left the remote possibility of Abe being tied to the FBI attacks on the lab or the assassination attempt in Bambari.

Abe jumped when his secure phone rang.

All his allies were dead. Who could this be? He opted for caution as he answered. "Hello."

"Abe, this is General Kuo."

Kuo wasn't dead, but he was on his way back to China to play it safe. Why would he be calling?

"General, I thought you would be gone by now."

"And I would have been except for some information I received from my intelligence people. The police found Marsh's body and are ruling it as a suicide. The note was very convincing."

"Thanks for confirming that. I hadn't heard anything this morning."

"Another thing my intelligence network told me is that Warrington has a video conference planned for this morning with Meiling Chen-Adams and her entire team."

"Where do you get this kind of intel, Kuo?"

"Never mind that. Just listen. They will all be at the lab this morning. So I have released a little gift that I have been holding for an appropriate time to give to them."

"A gift?"

"An Iranian drone called *Qods Ababil* with a thermobaric bomb as its payload. The lab, the people, and all those viruses will be vaporized. Maybe that is a slight exaggeration. At least they will be cremated."

"But what about the air defense system? Can the drone reach its target?"

"My people assembled it, and I launched it from a remote area near the Fort Peck Indian Reservation in

Northeastern Montana. The drone travels at one hundred eighty miles per hour, and it follows the terrain. Who is going to see it?" Kuo laughed. "If I could have, I would have done this months ago. And the best part is that these Iranian drones contain parts made by thirteen U.S. companies. Such irony." Kuo laughed again. "These Americans are fools."

Just when Abe thought everything might be slipping away, maybe there was hope. "When does the blessed event take place?"

"In less than two hours, 10:55 a.m. Mountain Time. And this is much more efficient than using the inept FBI agents that Harold Stein kept offering us."

"I hope you are right, general. And I hope all goes well for you back in Beijing or wherever you are going."

"And may you get your vaccine wishes, Abe. That will help your cause and mine too."

They ended the call.

***

Two hours later, 10:40 a.m. Mountain Daylight Time

After everyone sat, and the room quieted. The president's head filled the monitor on the wall.

"I have consolidated my recent reports from the State Department and DHHS. This clearly shows that we have the Novel Marburg Virus on the run. If we stay the current course, we can eradicate this insidious weapon of biowarfare in a few more months. The only question for my administration that remains: What reparations do we demand from China? Whatever we demand, I think the CCP will never end the development of bioweapons. Therefore, I am asking you to continue your work at Dr. Pierce's lab, and we will determine a new budget and resource allocation required to stay one step ahead of the CCP and PLA."

Meiling scanned the faces in the room. “Is anyone here not in favor of continuing our work?”

There was no reply.

“There is your answer, Warren.”

“Thank you, Meiling. The next matter involves the FBI pressing for custody of the arrested agents held by the Superior Police Department. This has led to the discovery of two high-ranking FBI members who are pushing the writ of *habeas corpus*. They are now on administrative leave and are being investigated. The Attorney General has stopped the writ and started the housecleaning of the DOJ. Dangers to you from our FBI are over.

“The third matter is the sabotaging of your mAbs sent to Bambari. Next week, Secretary of State James Wilson will present his findings on the pilots and two others in the State Department who were involved in the Bambari conspiracy. The four people involved will be indicted and likely charged with a long list of crimes.

“Just a moment.” The president paused, and he appeared to be scanning a document. “I have been informed that an unidentified drone was spotted early this morning by a B-52 crew on a low-level bombing run in Eastern Montana.

“It was seen crossing I-90 a few miles west of Cheyenne about thirty minutes ago. Now it’s less than ten minutes from the lab if that is, in fact, the target.”

Ryan took Meiling’s hand. “If it’s that close, there are no fighter squadrons within striking distance.”

The room went completely silent.

Chapter 29

10:45 a.m. Mountain Time, lab conference room

Baker laid his hand on Rafe's shoulder. "There are no fighters, but there is a Huey Cobra. Come on, Rafe. Let's go."

"Please leave your video on. I need to follow this development in real time," the president said.

Rafe and Baker sprinted out the door toward the Huey, sitting about one hundred and fifty yards away.

"Our only chance is to take it down with the Huey," Baker said as they ran toward the field ahead.

"What's its max speed?" Rafe said between breaths.

"A drone that size ... the max speed is probably about the same as our Huey. So, we can't run it down."

"Which means we have to take it straight on." Rafe shot a glance at Baker as they reached the Huey.

Baker nodded. "Yes, precisely straight on. Which means if we can't shoot it down—"

"Yeah," Rafe said. "We make it take us down."

They start to climb in.

"Wait, Baker. You've got a wife and kids, so—"

"No, you don't, Rafe. You've got a family too. We'll take this demon drone down together one way or another."

Baker buckled in.

Rafe started the engine, and it whined as it slowly revved up.

Now the wop, wop began.

"Seven minutes, Rafe. Let's get this Cobra off the ground."

The pulsating roar began, and the Huey tilted forward and rose into the air.

"You've got the controls, Rafe, so I'll be the gunner."

"What are you gonna use first?"

"Silly question, dude. The M129 grenade launcher."

"Baker, we'll be closing at over three hundred miles per hour."

"Yep. That's five miles a minute. I can start shooting a mile away. At one mile, that gives me about ten seconds and seventy grenades to take it down because we will collide in twelve seconds. If it explodes two seconds before the collision, I'm not sure the Huey can avoid the explosion, depending upon what's in the drone's payload."

"Then I shouldn't veer from collision course until we see the explosion."

"You got it, bro."

"You had a marksman ribbon in the military. You'd better shoot like a marksman, or ..."

"Yeah. Or."

"We're a mile out from the lab hovering over a huge field. This looks like a good place to make our stand. The worst thing that can happen on the ground is we start a grass fire."

The radio crackled then a voice came through Baker's headset. "This is Pearce. How's it going?"

"We're in position to take the drone down and have about three and a half minutes until I start firing," Baker said.

"Baker, this is Shauna. I love you. The girls and I are praying for you."

"You don't have to worry about you and the girls. We're facing down this incoming demon, and one way or another, it will go down."

A gasping sound came through Baker's headset. Shauna understood the stakes.

"Gotta go now, Shauna. I love you."

"Bro, can you see anything on the radar?" Rafe's voice.

"Not yet. The Cobra Radar System is good for about five miles. That covers the last minute before collision. I'll start firing at fifteen seconds, ending at five seconds. If you see an explosion, veer away. If not, stay the course."

"Got it," Rafe said. "Baker, is there any chance that drone can fly right through us and still reach the target?"

"Don't ask questions like that this late in the ga—hang on. The drone just entered radar range. Coming straight at us."

Baker tried to remain laser-focused on the radar and his gun controls. "Forty-five seconds. Maintain course, Rafe."

"Thirty seconds. The drone is turning to our left to avoid us."

"I'm on it, Baker."

With the drone turning to circle them, keeping the sights on it grew more difficult.

"Preparing to fire. Twenty seconds and ... firing."

A stream of grenades flew from the M129 grenade launcher in a rapid staccato rhythm.

Ten seconds.

Nine.

Eight. Baker kept pressure on the trigger.

Seven.

Six.

A flash temporarily blinded Baker.

Rafe banked and veered right.

The shock wave hit the underside of the Huey driving Baker down into his seat and thumping his head like a hammer.

Rafe fought the controls as their bird writhed in the wake of a shockwave from an enormous explosion. "We're going down, bro."

"No. Ease off the controls for two seconds, then go full throttle."

Rafe complied, and the Huey righted itself and then began climbing.

"In the nick of time, Rafe. I could count grass blades in that field. You kept us in the air after what I'm certain was a thermobaric weapon explosion. Whoever did this meant to destroy the entire lab complex." Baker paused. "Now, get us back to our landing spot by the lab so that we can check out our bird for damage?"

"Gladly," Rafe said.

Pierce's voice returned on the radio. "The whole building shook down here. Are you all okay?"

"Mission accomplished," Baker said. "Tell everybody we're okay and they are safe."

***

10:55 a.m.

Pierce scampered down the hallway and entered the conference room. "Baker and Rafe got the drone and are landing right now."

Cheers and clapping erupted as the emotions of the past few minutes washed away in a flood of relief.

The president's head appeared in the monitor. "Give Baker and Rafer Jackson my hearty congratulations for a job well done. The outcome was an answer to this man's prayer. But, folks, I am receiving another message, and it does seem to be of interest to you."

The president paused and was, apparently, reading the message. "This is something you all should know about. We have just verified that Abe Borland, CEO of Phisher Pharmaceuticals, was involved with Harold Stein at the FBI and with Marshall McDowell of the CDC in the attempts to end Meiling's team's management of the Marburg response.

"Marshall McDowell was found dead earlier today from an apparent suicide attempt, but the investigation of his death isn't yet complete.

"Abe Borland will be arrested and charged with multiple counts of murder, attempted murder, and violation of 18 U.S. Code § 2381, which is treason. Mr. Borland's actions allegedly violated the three key elements necessary for an offense to constitute treason: an obligation of allegiance to the legal order and the intent and action to violate that obligation. He has allegedly breached the faithful support a citizen owes to the nation within which he lives."

"He certainly had the most incentive to remove us from the Marburg response," Ryan said.

"But do not rule out CCP or PLA involvement," Lee said.

"Stein was assassinated. McDowell commits suicide," Ryan said. "I wonder what will happen to Abe Borland?"

***

11:00 a.m.

Abe turned on an all-news radio station known for being the first to report breaking news.

How long would he have to wait to hear about the drone taking out Pierce's lab?

His desk phone rang, and he answered.

"Mr. Borland, this is Debbie at the front desk. Something strange is happening here."

Abe's breath caught in his throat. He took a calming breath and cleared his throat. "What's that, Debbie?"

"Several police arrived, and they are headed for your office. Security may delay them, but the guard will eventually let them through."

"Thanks, Debbie." He ended the call.

So this was it. After all his effort and planning, this is how it would end.

But Abe was confident of one thing. It would not end with him in prison.

He unlocked his bottom desk drawer and placed his thumb on the gun safe. It whirred for a second and then opened.

Abe's hands shook as he struggled to pick up the .38 in the safe.

He held the gun to his head, then lowered it.

The sound of running feet came echoing down the hallway.

Abe had only seconds left.

He returned the gun barrel to his head. As he did, something or someone deep inside said, "Pull the trigger."

Abe complied.

Chapter 30

11:10 a.m., the lab conference room

Meiling sat in a chair at the conference room table.

Ryan sat beside her and took her hand.

The president appeared on the monitor again. "This has been a long morning for everyone. My DOJ and intelligence organizations are tracking down the participants in the drone attack. Please do not touch any of the debris from the drone explosion. FBI from the Colorado Field Office will arrive shortly to examine it."

He paused. "Do you folks have any questions before we end this video meeting?"

Ming nodded toward Meiling. "You tell him, Meiling."

"Okay. Mr. President—"

"Don't you mean Warren?" He smiled warmly.

"No. This is an issue for Mr. President. The team believes we need an independent panel of scientists to develop recommendations for any future use of mRNA vaccines or treatments such as those rumored to be under development by Phisher Pharmaceuticals and Mercer Medical.

"We need to prevent repeating the disasters experienced during the COVID pandemic. The use of mRNA injections or infusions must be restricted to the small set of services for which they are appropriate, and they must never again be equated with vaccines.

"This will tell the pharmaceutical corporations, loud and clear, that they cannot make money from mRNA vaccines. Conveying that message should end the misuse and abuse of that potentially dangerous technology."

"May I allow my Press Secretary, Kate Williams, to convey your words to the media?"

"If you agree, yes. But I suggest that you already have the panel chosen before you reveal your intent. Otherwise, you will have unethical scientists and bureaucrats clamoring to get on the panel—people like we have seen directing previous pandemic responses."

"I see what you mean, Meiling."

"If a person really wants to save people's lives, then they cannot pursue money, power, or glory. And, Mr. President, we should only quarantine the sick, not the healthy. Furthermore, we should introduce legislation to change required vaccinations to recommendations, always allowing exemptions for valid reasons and reasonable alternative medical interventions."

"I agree, Meiling, but there are other related issues. For instance, the infiltration of the CCP into almost every aspect of our society, industry, and education. We must deal with that issue."

"Those are matters for your intelligence agencies."

"Agencies which I can't always trust. They try to manipulate my decisions by the selective revelation of intelligence. At some point, the CCP will try to capitalize on all they've set up here in the U.S. They will make some kind of power play."

"If the CCP wanted to make an aggressive move, they could always release a deadly virus to create the needed chaos."

"And that's why I need you to continue your work at Pierce's lab."

"And we have agreed to do that. But for that effort, there is intel that we need but aren't privy to. And I have lost all my contacts at Wuhan—well, I haven't exactly lost them. They are here working with me now."

"Meiling, I can clear you and your team and splice them into our intel network, so you receive periodic briefings. I can do that by allowing you access only to what you need to accomplish your goals."

"Which goals would those be?"

"To thwart all attempts to use biowarfare weapons on this nation." He paused. "Now, is that all, Meiling?" The president gave her a crooked smile.

"No. We must never allow the bureaucrats to prevent a doctor from using approved drugs for off-label treatments."

"You don't seem to have a very high opinion of our medical bureaucrats, Meiling."

"No. They have tried to take away my right to practice medicine and prevent me from using proven treatments that can save millions of people's lives. Would you, Mr. President, have a high opinion of such people? They are the demagogues of darkness. They are those we are at war with as we fight against the darkness in America."

President Warrington sighed loud and long. "As long as there are people on this earth with darkened hearts, there will be darkness and a need for light."

Lee had slipped quietly beside Meiling. He laid a hand on her shoulder. "Mr. President, I was a manifested Maoist for many decades, steeped in darkness, knowing neither what I was missing nor the evil I was evoking. Then, Meiling saved my life. At this lab, I found life, light, love, and acceptance when Ryan Adams introduced me to Jesus. And those who work here showed me how to follow him. Perhaps some of your medical bureaucrats should spend some time working with us."

"Perhaps they should, Dr. Li. Perhaps they should."

The president ended the video meeting, and the tired team members began filing out of the conference room.

Ryan stopped Meiling when she turned toward the door. He wrapped her up snugly in his strong arms. "The first three months of your pregnancy have been filled with more challenges than most women could survive. It's time for you to get some rest, get enough sleep, and watch your diet. In a little less than six months—"

"I know, sweetheart. I will get more rest. But we must not give up our fight for truth and light in this nation because we will be raising our daughter here. I want her to see something that most Chinese alive today have never known—a nation where the light of truth and liberty shines so brightly that it chases away ***the darkness within***."

Author's Notes

The Darkness Within focuses on the growing evil within the healthcare industry and its administration by bureaucrats in the federal and state governments. This trend of unethical and immoral practices reveals profiteering and blatant disregard for the lives and health of patients. The COVID Pandemic exposed this more than any previous failures. I believe that healthcare in the U.S. will never be the same and that Americans' trust in the system and in their doctors has been permanently damaged.

On a lighter note, I thoroughly enjoyed bringing back to life in this story the Vietnam Era attack helicopter, the Huey Cobra. Its peculiar, pulsating, whirring roar was a welcome sound to many young American men pinned down by Viet Cong gunfire. For its time, the Cobra was a fierce and feared weapon. You saw that in my story by the devastation it wrought in only a few seconds.

With great sadness, I painted a tainted picture of what used to be America's elite law enforcement arm of the Department of Justice (DOJ), the FBI. Much of the DOJ has been politically weaponized to the point that American citizens can no longer expect justice if they are accused of a crime or have been victimized by criminals. The injustice is often carried out by members of the FBI. Its motto, Fidelity, Bravery, Integrity, no longer applies. Many people are calling to disband the FBI and start another organization from scratch.

The Darkness Within was set a few years into the future. As such, the doctors in the story looked back on the COVID-19 Pandemic to glean what they could for the Novel Marburg Pandemic. You undoubtedly noted that my characters spoke disparagingly of the policies for handling COVID-19 and of the mRNA "***vaccines***" forced upon much of the earth's population.

Now, evidence surfacing daily vindicates this view of the COVID pandemic's policies and vaccines. Huge excess mortality exists in nations that were highly vaccinated. It cannot be explained in any other way than the vaccines. These data come from life insurance companies, and we know that the actuaries—statisticians who determine the premiums for the insurance policies—are the most reliable statisticians on the planet. They rarely make mistakes. Yet these insurance companies are paying out enormous sums of money to the families of people who statistically should never have died.

In my story, Meiling used mRNA injections or infusions but only to introduce a protein that would kill a targeted pathogen, not to induce immunity. Even with this approach, she detoxed her patients to remove the mRNA from the patients' bodies once she had sufficiently reduced the viral load. She did this to eliminate any chance of damage to their immune systems from the foreign mRNA running loose and replicating in the cells of their bodies.

The Gulfstream G550 that Baker flies is an incredible machine. The missile avoidance systems in the story do exist and have been added to some G550s. For example, in Israel, because of the danger from terrorists, missile avoidance is often added to this airplane.

I do not know if there will be a book 4 in this series. That depends on actions by the big pharmaceutical companies, government bureaucrats, and possibly on the 2024 election.

If you enjoyed *The Darkness Within*, please leave a review on Amazon for this book.
https://www.amazon.com/stores/author/B00B1XMR56

This helps other readers find books they will enjoy and is a wonderful way to encourage the author. You can reach me on Facebook as H L Wegley or Harry Wegley or through my author website:
https://www.hlwegley.com

To read the prologue from book 1 of my previous series, Riven Republic, go to the next page.

https://www.amazon.com/Riven-Republic-Book-1-ebook/dp/B085NBQ3WL

Riven Prologue

Zach Tanner drew a long breath as he sat in his chair in the Rogue Valley's KROG-AM studio. The clock said only two minutes remained in his network program, Zach's Facts. He leaned toward the mixing console, placing his mouth an inch from the mic, and began his closing remarks in a low, unrelenting voice.

"America may not be where it was on March 4, 1861, when Abraham Lincoln was inaugurated. But many of the divisions that led to that terrible Civil War exist today—divided views of our national history, divided views of our founding documents, of our monuments, of most of our symbols, of what it means to be a patriot, and what it means to be an American."

Propelled by the driving rhythm of his heart, the words pulsated from his lips.

"We are in a cold civil war, but one that will grow hot given the slightest provocation. I believe many provocations are coming, and the incompatible political ideologies on the right and the left prevent any resolution but a violent one, a rending of our nation. It will not play out as it did in 1861, but every American will know that we are at war when one group crosses the line, a point of no return, leaving a riven republic. And as the nation fragments in a *de facto* secession and struggles against itself, the question on each true American heart is, can we ever recover what we once had?

"The courts cannot save us from ourselves. No part of the federal government can. Maybe if enough pulpits echo the call to revival, God will move as He has in the past. Maybe the hearts and minds of millions will be changed, and we will find unity once again.

"At this critical juncture in American history, it appears that only an act of God can save this nation. May God have mercy on the United States of America."

Zach hit the button that played the closing theme for his show.

How much longer could he endure painting gut-wrenching pictures of the state of our severance to the citizens of the nation he loved, a nation barreling headlong into a tunnel of total darkness?

And how much longer until I'm arrested for doing this?

https://www.amazon.com/Riven-Republic-Book-1-ebook/dp/B085NBQ3WL

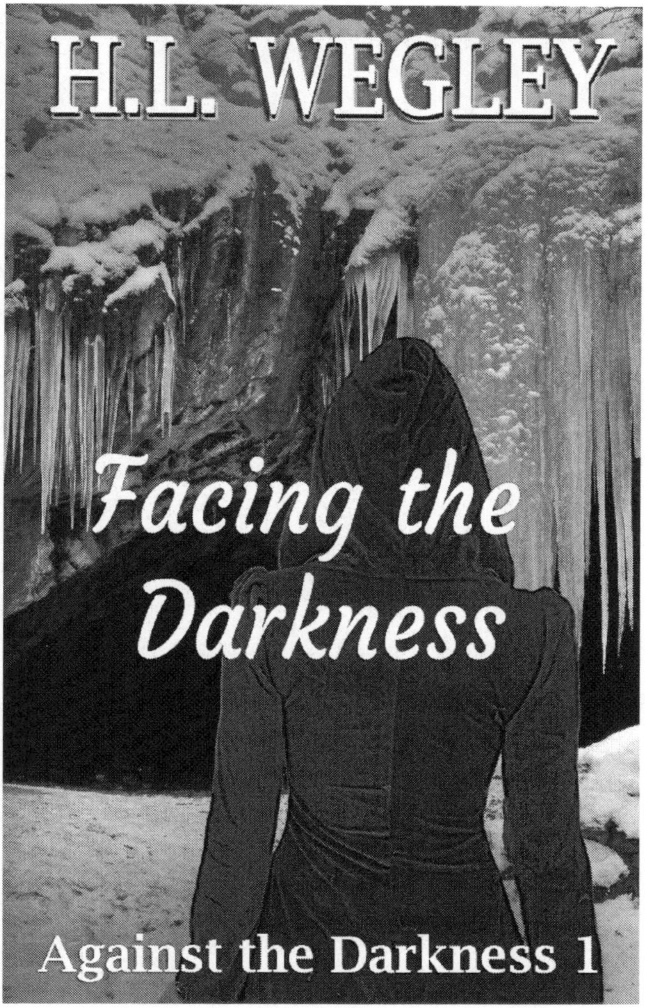

https://www.amazon.com/stores/H.-L.-Wegley/author/B00B1XMR56

https://www.amazon.com/stores/H.-L.-Wegley/author/B00B1XMR56

Made in the USA
Columbia, SC
05 April 2023

14578163R00124